THE GHOST IN THE GAZEBO:

AN ANTHOLOGY OF NEW ENGLAND GHOST STORIES

Edited

by

Edward Lodi

Rock Village Publishing
41 Walnut Street
Middleborough MA 02346
(508) 946-4738

THE GHOST IN THE GAZEBO:

AN ANTHOLOGY OF NEW ENGLAND GHOST STORIES

Edited

by

Edward Lodi

Rock Village Publishing
Middleborough, Massachusetts

First Printing

ISBN 0-9721389-1-9

This book is dedicated to

Ruth Brown

Artist, typographer, friend

ACKNOWLEDGMENTS

"Old Rex" by Joy V. Smith has seen publication in
The Sixth Sense Anthology (1998) and *Classic Pulp
Fiction Stories* (1999) and online in *Anotherealm* (2000).

"Waiting for Mr. Eldredge" by Charles Danzoll
originally appeared in 1979 as a privately printed
chapbook.

"Charlie" by Barbara Brent Brower was first published
in the Australian literary magazine, *Tirra Lirra*.

"More Than Music" by Lenora K. Rogers was originally
published in *Cemetery Sonata II* in October, 2000.

"The Chill of an Early Fall" by Terry Campbell first
saw publication in the December 1993 issue of
Gathering Darkness.

CONTENTS

INTRODUCTION

Of the hundreds of volumes of ghost stories that litter the shelves, spill onto the floor, and otherwise clutter up our house (driving my long-suffering wife to distraction), my favorite bears the title *Shapes That Haunt the Dusk*. So enamored am I of this little tome that I came up with variations of its title for two collections of my own, *Shapes That Haunt New England* and *Haunters of the Dusk*.

Published by Harpers & Brothers in 1907, *Shapes That Haunt the Dusk* contains ten short stories. One reason why I value them so much, other than the fact that they are for the most part exceptionably well written, is their almost total obscurity. Many of the ghost books that fill up my shelves are redundant; dozens of the stories they contain—scores, actually—are repeated in one or more collections. Not so with *Shapes That Haunt the Dusk*. Even the names of the authors—with the possible exception of Howard Pyle, who is still vaguely remembered (though perhaps more for his drawings and illustrations than for his books)—have with the passage of time, like the phantoms they wrote of, become pale and thin and for the most part forgotten.

A pity: that so many splendidly written ghost stories should languish in dust and go largely unread by aficionados of the genre. It's a fate that, but for a chance visit to a used bookstore on Cape Cod, might have befallen one of the stories contained within this present collection.

A Gathering Place is a cozy little bookstore in Dennis, on scenic Route 6A just before the intersection with Route 134. It's a nice place in which to browse. But the reason why I stopped by that fateful day was not so much to seek out books as to visit Details, my favorite bookstore cat—a friendly feline of exceptional intellect who has the virtue of being always present, though never underfoot.

After greeting Details and chatting with the proprietor, Karen Nowell, for a while, I browsed around and found a book (for once not a collection of ghost stories) that I wanted to buy. I plunked it down on the counter prefatory to paying for it. And there, staring me in the face so to speak, lay a slim chapbook, yellow with age but in otherwise pristine condition, titled "Waiting for Mr. Eldredge" and subtitled "A Ghost Story."

I picked it up, saw that it was nicely illustrated, and despite the impossibly tiny print, immediately bought it (for the princely sum of seventy-five cents). "Oh, that came in a couple of days ago," Karen said, when I commented on the unlikely circumstance of finding it right there on the counter. As soon as I got home that evening I began to read it, with—seeing that it was privately printed—low expectations. How pleasantly surprised, then, to find myself immediately drawn into the story and mesmerized by the eerie atmosphere and the narrator's vivid descriptions of the Maine coast.

For some time I'd been toying with the idea of editing an anthology of ghost stories with New England settings. "Waiting for Mr. Eldredge" convinced me to go ahead with the project. It would provide the perfect centerpiece for the book.

That is, if I could track down the author and secure his permission to reprint the story, which first saw publication in 1979.

Fortunately my wife, who understands the intricacies of the Internet far better than I ever will, was able to come up with the address and phone number of Charles Danzoll who, as author of "Waiting for Mr. Eldredge," had it privately printed in Connecticut in the form of a chapbook nearly a quarter of a century ago—and who apparently was taken completely by surprise upon receiving my phone call requesting permission to resurrect it from the dead for inclusion in this anthology.

The chapbook, I learned, has an interesting history. Before "Waiting for Mr. Eldredge" was written, its basic story was narrated by Charles Danzoll to his two boys around a campfire in Maine early one summer evening. The three of them were sitting around the campfire, after hot-dogs and marshmallows. Before them was an island: "Above the ledges and shoreline, there rose the familiar masses of dark green spruce trees, so tightly packed one wondered how anything—man or beast—could force its way through."

"Writing the story," Charles Danzoll says, "after its somewhat hesitant and inept oral debut, and producing the booklet, was a fun affair. A friend typed the manuscript; another created drawings that illustrated key events in the story; a third friend, who worked in the Print department of my company, produced 200 booklets of the story for free. These booklets were sent to family friends and distributed to schoolmates of the two boys. The story was studied in their classes and became the subject of at least two school assemblies in which I participated as a 'new local author.' "

Don't be deceived by the story's humble origin. "Waiting for Mr. Eldredge" far transcends the "told-around-a-campfire" sub-genre of ghost story. I predict that "Mr. Eldredge" will be around, in one form or another, for many years to come.

Never one to pass up an opportunity to share a worthy piece of writing, let me quote, at length, from William Dean Howells's introduction to *Shapes That Haunt the Dusk*. The words he wrote in praise of the stories he included in his anthology apply equally well to the stories I have chosen to include in mine.

"The writers of American short stories, the best short stories in the world, surpass in nothing so much as in their handling of those filmy textures which clothe the vague shapes of the borderland between experience and illusion. This is perhaps because our people, who seem to live only in the most tangible things of material existence, really live more in the spirit than any other. Their love of the supernatural is their common inheritance from no particular ancestry, but is apparently an effect from psychological influences in the past, widely separated in time and space. It is as noticeable among our Southerners of French race as among our New Englanders deriving from Puritan zealots accustomed to wonder-working providences, or among those descendants of the German immigrants who brought with them to our Middle States the superstitions of the Rhine valleys or the Hartz mountains. It is something that has tinged the nature of our whole life, whatever its varied sources, and when its color seems gone out of us, or, going, it renews itself in all the mystical lights and shadows so familiar to us that; till we read some such tales as those grouped together here, we are scarcely aware how largely they form the complexion of our thinking and feeling."

Howells concludes his introduction: "Such as they severally and differently and collectively are, the pieces are each a masterpiece and worthy the study of every reader who feels that there are more things than we have dreamt of in our philosophy.

The collection is like a group of immortelles, gray in that twilight of the reason which Americans are so fond of inviting, or, rather, they are like a cluster of Indian pipe, those pale blossoms of the woods that spring from the dark mould in the deepest shade, and are so entirely of our own soil."

With one exception, all of the masterpieces in *The Ghost in the Gazebo* take place in New England. And all of them, again with one exception, are works of fiction. In both instances the one exception is Barbara Brent Brower's "Charlie," the true story of a ghostly encounter that took place in the state of Maryland.

Some eighty years ago William Allen White—himself an editor—wrote: "Consistency is a paste jewel that only cheap men cherish." Not wishing to be labeled "cheap," I have chosen to include "Charlie" in this collection of fictional New England ghost stories because...well, because fortuitously it came my way and is very nicely written, and because it serves to remind us that hauntings—often dismissed by dullards as mere figments of the imagination—can be very real, indeed.

So "Charlie" isn't fiction? So its setting isn't New England? So sue me.

But I warn you. One of the excellent writers whose stories are contained herein—Sarah C. Honenberger— is an attorney. If sued, I will ask her to defend me. If she brings to my defense only a small fraction of the consummate skill she brought to "The Lodge," my case is already won.

All of the stories presented in this anthology are superb, of course; otherwise I would not have chosen them. Several are reprints, having originally been published in literary journals or anthologies with excellent reputations but often limited readerships. Others appear here for the very first time. I wish that I could boast of having discovered a brilliant new talent, that here for the first time ever is introduced the work of a previously unknown writer. But no. Each of the writers whose stories are represented in *The Ghost in the Gazebo* has a proven track record, some more extensive than others, perhaps, but all of them impressive.

Christopher Conlon, for instance. Chris graciously sent along copies of some of his published work, including *California Sorcery*, an anthology containing stories by the writers known as The Group—including such giants in their field as Charles Beaumont, Robert Block, Richard Matheson, and Ray Bradbury, to name but a few—edited by William F. Nolan and William Schafer, for which Chris wrote the (extensive) introduction. I was so impressed by the quality of Christopher Conlon's writing that I was almost tempted to turn over to him the task of editing *this* anthology. (But...given his obviously keen intelligence and discerning judgment, he might very well have chosen to exclude the title story—my own contribution!)

Or Dianalee Velie. Dianalee has not only published in more places than most writers even get around to just submitting to, but also her poems, stories, and plays have won so many honors it would take a second volume of this anthology just to list them.

Then of course there's Scott Thomas...D. K. McCutchen... Terry Campbell.

Maria Pollack...Joy V. Smith...Lenora K. Rogers.

I could go on and on, citing all of the authors individually, and ringing their praises. But doing so might prove redundant, insofar as a brief author's biography precedes each story. And I'd run the risk of sounding like a proud grandparent bragging about his grandkids' many accomplishments. See how beautifully written they all are! See how this one is thrilling, this one uplifting, this one thought-provoking, this one terrifying. See how this one leaves you glancing over your shoulder, reluctant after dark to walk alone down a deserted street, or to put out the bedroom light at night.

In the end, of course, the stories need no assist; they speak for themselves. Though they are all different from one another—in plot, theme, mood, length, and intent of the author to frighten or mystify—they have this in common: they are the best of their genre. I say so unabashedly, proud grandparent after all.

Immortelle: a plant with flowers that retain their color when dried.

Indian pipe: a saprophytic woodland plant. Also known as the *corpse-plant*, for its waxy whiteness, and the fact that, lacking green chlorophyll, it derives its nourishment from dead and decaying organic matter in the forest shade. (Despite its associations with death, Indian pipe is a delicate flower of more than passing beauty. It grows abundantly on the three and one-half acres of New England soil I call home, and I take care never to tread upon it.)

Each and every one of the stories contained within *The Ghost in the Gazebo* will, I assure you, thrive in the shade and fertile soil of your imagination. And will resonate—retain its color—long after the reading. ◊

The Ghost in the Gazebo
Edward Lodi

Edward Lodi taught English at the Massachusetts Maritime Academy in Buzzards Bay and at Shaw University in Raleigh, North Carolina (where he took an active part in the Civil Rights Movement of the 1960's); trained social workers for the Massachusetts Division of Medical Assistance; and was himself employed as a social worker for the Department of Public Welfare. He is the author of eight books, three of them collections of ghost stories.

With hindsight the drowning—like most tragic mishaps—might easily have been avoided. If only he had taken rudimentary precautions...

The afternoon junket had been on the spur-of-the-moment, a sudden whim. By rights he should have tossed a life preserver into the boat. And paid closer attention to the weather. But languor—a lassitude induced by the pleasures of that long, hot, lazy summer—together with increasing prowess with the sailboat, had caused him to grow careless. He ignored what should have been obvious warning signs: the darkening sky, the freshening wind, the whitecaps frolicking like wanton mermaids in the open harbor.

The sudden squall caught him unawares.

Even when the capsized boat drifted hopelessly out of reach Jonathan did not become unduly alarmed. He was, after all, a skilled swimmer. And young, sixteen years old, much too young to die. As he struggled against the current, the undertow that robbed him of his strength—as he thrashed to keep his head above the salt waves that stung his eyes and sucked away his breath—he kept his gaze firmly fixed on the receding shore, on the weathercock perched high atop the belvedere.

Even though the octagonal structure seemed to teeter on the rim of the lawn's broad sweep, Jonathan knew that as long as he kept the copper weathercock and the belvedere's profile firmly in view he could make it to shore. He *would* make it to shore, he promised himself, even as the current churned and sucked him under, into the channel and out to sea.

In the end Jonathan kept his promise. In the end he made it, all the way to shore and into the belvedere.

When, two days after the drowning, fishermen retrieved Jonathan's body from the bottom of Buzzards Bay, they carried it across the lawn and into the belvedere, where they laid it out on the floor before proceeding on up to notify the folks in the big house.

In time the belvedere gained a reputation for being haunted. Jonathan's ghost, people said, could be seen, on certain summer afternoons or stormy evenings, gazing out onto the lawn or up toward the big house, his pale, gaunt face, wedged between his hands, pressed hard against the screens—like someone trapped inside, like someone longing to break free.

For her granddaughter's sixteenth birthday—on the twenty-third of July—Marcella Owens threw a party on the grounds of her seaside estate. Only close friends —including a handful of select neighbors—and family members (of varying degrees of consanguinity) were invited. Even so, by mid afternoon nearly sixty guests loitered or lounged in scattered clumps down by the beach or near the food pavilion which the caterers had set up, shortly after dawn, midway between house and ocean.

There was to be dancing in the evening, for which a local jazz group had been commissioned. For now, though, in the heat of day, food would be the major attraction and after that, tennis, croquet, swimming, or—for the less athletic—sunbathing or whist.

Alcoholic beverages—beer and wine—would not be available until after five p.m. For the dispensing of drinks, Mrs. Owens had engaged the services of professional bartenders, a married couple of middle age with a reputation for clearheadedness: for refusing to serve alcoholic drinks to underage guests, and for seeing to it that guests of legal drinking age did not overindulge. Mrs. Owens did not disapprove of alcohol; she was by no means a teetotaler; she enjoyed a glass of chardonnay or merlot with dinner. But she was mindful of the dangers that alcohol posed—in particular for two or three of her guests, blood relations whom she'd invited out of necessity, rather than by choice.

One of these guests of dubious distinction was her grandnephew, Kevin. Although only twenty-one years of age, the young man had already been kicked out of two ivy-league colleges. That he was presently enrolled in a third was a tribute not to any academic or athletic abilities he might possess, but to the fact that his deceased granduncle, Marcella Owens's half-brother, had generously endowed the school library. Kevin Cowles was an irresponsible, impetuous youth with—at least to Mrs. Owens's way of thinking—few redeeming qualities.

It was for this reason that at the earliest opportunity she drew him to one side and requested a word with him.

"Shall we go and sit in the belvedere, where it's quiet?" she asked. It was more command than request.

Somewhat bemused (he'd obviously been smoking something: pot, or grass, or whatever name they gave to it these days) he followed her aside and into the ancient screened-in structure, and took a seat on the bench opposite to the one upon which she plunked herself.

"I'm cutting you out of my will," she told him bluntly, without preamble. "I thought it only fair to let you know."

He stared at her—rather stupidly, she thought.

"Why, Aunt Marcie," he finally said with an acidic grin, just when she'd begun to suspect he'd fallen into some sort of cataleptic trance, "I never knew you'd included me in the first place. It was thoughtful of you, though."

She glared back at him. "Don't be asinine, Kevin. I did include you but now I'm cutting you out, completely. I'm sure the last thing you want from me right now is a lecture so I'll spare you one. I will say this much: you're young, and you may yet mend your ways. Though I seriously doubt it."

When he said nothing in reply but simply sat there, grinning, she got up to leave. "And one other thing. I've instructed the bartenders to serve you only non-alcoholic beverages—although I suspect you have at hand your own means of befuddling your mind."

She unlatched the screen door and stepped incongruously onto the carpet of soft grass which, despite a recent drought (and because of the frequent morning mists and heavy fogs that drifted in from the bay), remained green throughout the hot summer months. Leaving her grandnephew to his own devices, she went off in search of her granddaughter.

Kevin remained seated for another ten minutes, breathing in the fresh air and marveling at the wonders of nature: at the blue water, at the way sunlight glinted off its hard surface like flakes of diamonds. At the way the terns pirouetted above the waves like whorls of whittled wood.

Shit, he suddenly realized: *whorls of whittled wood*. Deep down inside he was a poet. He had beautiful—he had *insightful*—thoughts. His great aunt didn't realize that. Nobody realized that. Someday he'd write a book. In the meantime...

Feeling a hunger that was more spiritual than physical, he swung through the doorway onto the lawn and joined the crowd in search of sustenance.

Marcella Owens spotted her granddaughter by the boat ramp chatting with a group of girls from school. Not wishing to tear the child away from her friends, Marcella waited until they had begun to gravitate toward the pavilion before drawing her aside. Seeing that the belvedere was once again empty, she opted to speak to Sherri there.

Bored equally with the gathering and with himself, Kevin sat at a table in the shade of an umbrella trying to decide whether he should get up and leave—and thereby risk the finality of burning all his bridges—or remain at the party, in hopes that he might somehow, someday, regain his great aunt's good graces, to the extent that she might, sometime before her belated death, relent and throw a measly buck or two his way.

Out of the corner of his eye he watched his young cousin being led into the gazebo—the screened-in summerhouse which his great aunt persisted in calling by its old-fashioned name of *belvedere*.

What was going on? Had his little cousin been misbehaving? Was she, too, getting the ol' heave-ho?

Of course not. Aunt Marcie would hardly throw her granddaughter an elaborate birthday bash only to turn around and disinherit her.

Oops! Whatever grandma was saying must be to Sherri's liking, for just then the little wench leapt up from the bench (Hey! That rhymes!), tossed her arms around the old gal's neck, and planted a wet kiss on her wrinkled puss.

Kevin was sitting much too far away to hear what they were saying, but not so far as not to catch a glimpse of his cousin's lithe figure as she bounced up and embraced her grandmother. Sherri, he noticed—for the first time—was rather comely, in a nubile sort of way. Admittedly hers was a comeliness that would with time (a rather short time) diminish to drab frumpiness. Most adolescent girls—the vast majority—shared a first blush of... perhaps not *beauty* exactly. But at least something that was more than mere sex appeal. Of course, the pity was that whatever it was they shared didn't, in most cases, last more than a few years, in some cases less than a decade.

Poor Sherri, alas, when no longer *a lass* (hey, not bad for a budding poet!)... uh, where was he? Oh, yeah, cousin Sherri's looks (fair to middling to begin with) would not, he feared, pass the acid test of time. Her inherent *plainness* would, long before her thirtieth birthday, manifest itself all *too plainly*.

For now, however, she was "sweet sixteen." With all the trimmings.

What she might look like in a half dozen years was hardly germane to the scheme that, even now, was half-formed in his mind.

It wasn't until some two or three hours later—which was

just as well, since it allowed time for his mind to clear—it wasn't until a quarter past seven that Kevin saw an opportunity, and seized it, of getting his cousin off to one side, just the two of them, for a little tête-à-tête.

S herri Ferrioli had been aware for some time that a cousin of hers—a *distant* cousin (a second or third cousin, once- or perhaps even *twice*-removed, and a half relationship to boot)— had been eyeing her. Since childhood she'd known Kevin, mostly from meeting him at various family gatherings; she'd heard stories (rumors really): that he was wild and irresponsible, that he drank, that he experimented with drugs. Because of the infrequency of their meetings, and the considerable age difference—five years— they'd never had very much to say to one another.

However, as a person grew older—and more mature—a few years discrepancy seemed hardly important. And why in the world—in America of all places, where innocence is presumed until proved otherwise—why would an intelligent person ever lend credence to vicious gossip?

Furtively she checked him out. Not bad looking, if you disregarded his ears, which were just a wee bit too large. And he was not at all dissipated-looking. But wasn't that the way of the world: people always had nasty things to say about others whom they were jealous of. *Well of course*, she chided herself, *I'm biased, since he's constantly glancing my way.* But no, he didn't seem to her to be the least bit dissolute, or debauched, or whatever.

This was her sixteenth birthday. And—she reminded herself—she was a very mature sixteen. Weren't her teachers and for that matter her parents (away on a trip to Europe until next spring) always complimenting her on her good judgment and common sense? Why shouldn't an older guy (an intelligent, *good-looking* college student who did not—like so many of the boys she knew from private school—lead a dull or boring life)... why shouldn't a guy like Kevin Cowles find her attractive?

Heidi and Kathy had long ago wandered off toward the beach. She was beginning to wonder about those two...

Just why had they chosen *her* as a friend?

She was beginning to feel restless.

The band had begun playing the old-fashioned jazz that Sherri, knowing her grandmother's tastes, had chosen for her party. She could have selected something more to her own liking—something more contemporary—but the kind of music *she* liked would not have pleased her grandmother, nor for that matter most of the other guests, with the possible exception of Heidi and Kathy and one or two other friends from school.

"How's it going, cuz?" Kevin broke into her reverie and sat down beside her in the chair not too recently vacated by Kathy. "Nice party."

"Do you really mean that?" she heard herself say.

He hesitated, as if caught off guard by her cynicism, then countered with a judicious nod of his head. "Yeah. I like the music and the setting and the food. And the company's not bad. Why? You bored?"

"I was."

"But not now?"

"Not now," she said.

Kevin grinned inwardly. So it was going to be as easy as this.

"Mind if we go sit in the gazebo?" he asked after they'd chatted a bit. "It's getting buggy here."

She answered by rising from her seat. They strolled across the lawn, amiably, as if walking together was a practice of years' standing. All the others, it seemed, had gathered near the band, or still lingered by the food pavilion, or had sought out quiet spots on the beach. The light was beginning to thicken now; the sky above the water had taken on a dull cast; the wavelets lapping the shore shone with a metallic hue.

"Oh, it's occupied," Sherri said, disappointed.

Kevin paused to squint across the hundred or so feet that separated them from the gazebo. Other than the weathervane—a beaten-up rooster, coated with a century's worth of verdigris, perched high atop the roof—there was not a creature in sight.

"It doesn't appear to be," he said. "In fact it looks quite empty."

"I could swear I saw someone inside, looking out at us," Sherri said, puzzled. "A face." Then with a laugh added: "Maybe it's the ghost. It's supposed to be haunted."

"The gazebo?"

"That's what Tom, the old man who used to mow the lawn when I was little, used to tell me. And I've heard it from others. My grandmother, naturally, scoffs at the notion. But wouldn't it be fun if it was haunted!"

Kevin shuddered. He was not superstitious, exactly. Who in the twenty-first century would be? Even so he found the idea of ghosts distasteful. As a kid he'd been afraid of the dark. He still was, to some extent, though of course he'd never admit it, not even to himself.

"Sure," he replied. "A ghost would be amusing." As they entered the (thankfully deserted) gazebo he changed the subject.

Marcella Owens momentarily left off her duties as hostess in order to go off in search of her granddaughter, whom she'd last had a glimpse of shortly before dusk. As guest of honor, the child really should circulate more, or at least remain accessible.

She was not at all pleased when, after an exhaustive traverse of the grounds, she spotted Sherri in the belvedere with Kevin.

Kevin, on the other hand—given the circumstances—was very much pleased when his cousin imparted to him (in strictest confidence) her little secret, a secret which she had herself been told only that very day: that she was to be her grandmother's principal heir. That she, Sherri Ferrioli, would one day inherit the seaside mansion with all its grounds, including the very gazebo in which they were now seated.

It was upon hearing this good news that Kevin began his courtship in earnest.

Marcella knew better than to oppose her granddaughter's sudden and improbable infatuation with her worthless grandnephew. The girl—scarcely more than a child—would in time (a matter of months, if not weeks) come to her senses. Of that there could be no doubt. A sensible young woman, Sherri would soon see Kevin for what he was: a conniving, self-pitying milksop.

Marcella would not forbid Sherri to see him, nor would she discourage his visits to the house. The season was brief. Let the child have her summer romance, and be done with it.

In the meantime she—Marcella—would keep a close watch on the two of them.

By the end of August Kevin had established himself as a regular visitor to the ancestral house-by-the-sea. Although they did not admit to being more than just friends, Kevin seemed to dote on Sherri, and she on him.

Oh well, Marcella reflected one afternoon when the young people, leaving the old lady to her own devices, had maundered across the lawn down to the beach for a stroll along the water's edge; in less than a month Kevin would be returning to school. As would Sherri—who nonetheless would continue to reside with her grandmother, since the private school she attended was located in a neighboring town. Marcella doubted very much, in regards to the budding romance, that absence would make the heart grow fonder. On the contrary: she was confident that Kevin out of sight would soon be Kevin out of mind. Marcella knew about these things. She'd been young, once, herself.

While Marcella sat "by her lonesome" reading a book and enjoying the ninety degree weather— regardless of thermometer readings the air inside the belvedere never felt other than cool (according to her superstitious friends it was a preternatural cold, attributable to the presence of a ghost; Marcella of course scoffed at the notion)—Sherri likewise sat alone, on a granite outcrop overlooking the harbor. By tacit agreement, whenever he wanted "a smoke" Kevin would leave her and walk on ahead and out of sight. Sherri was not so naive as to imagine that these "smokes" of Kevin's always consisted of tobacco products. Though she herself did not do drugs, she saw no harm in Kevin's occasional use of marijuana. He was, after all, an adult. And everyone knows that the laws in this country pertaining to drugs are absolutely ridiculous.

And yet—if the truth be told she sometimes felt perturbed, even a tiny bit hurt, that being with her he so often felt the need to get high. Shouldn't the love for her that he so fervently professed be stimulant enough? (His answer, that she so turned him on that he had to take something as a substitute for the physical love that, so far, she cruelly denied him, didn't ring true. From what she'd read, and been told, marijuana intensified rather than diminished the desire for sex.)

It was therefore with only the slightest compunction that, upon hearing a faint, ominous rumble and noting a discoloration in the sky over the ocean, she slid down from the outcrop and began to make her way along the sand back toward the house. From experience she knew just how quickly the weather on Buzzards Bay could turn nasty. Let Kevin get caught in the storm without her. It would serve him right. Lately he'd been taking her far too much for granted.

Preceded by a brilliant flash, a loud clap shook the belvedere's wooden frame. The first hesitant drops began to strike against the roof. Seeing her granddaughter hurrying up from the beach, Marcella tucked the book under her arm and leaving the belvedere crossed the lawn to meet the child halfway. Together under blackening skies they skirted the gazebo and gained the shelter of the house seconds before the first downpour.

Although peeved to discover that Sherri had not waited for him at the rock, Kevin dismissed her truancy with a shrug. From the looks and sounds of it they were in for a really bad tempest; he could hardly blame the little twerp for not wanting to get soaked. Even so, how romantic it would have been: dashing for cover together. There! the poet in him again!

He strode deliberately but not too briskly across the firm sand. No need to run. He wasn't afraid of a little rain. Besides, presenting himself at Aunt Marcie's door in a thoroughly bedraggled state might invoke within her feelings of pity, might make her think more kindly of him.

As the skies darkened and the lightening began to flash in earnest he quickened his pace. From the base of the lawn he could clearly make out the gazebo and the pale outline of a face peering down in the direction of the beach. So little Sherri was on the lookout, anxious for his safety after all! He'd chide her for her desertion—then turn her feelings of guilt to his advantage.

With an air of nonchalance and, he hoped, bravado he disregarded the torrential rains that abruptly fell from the sky and made a leisurely beeline for the gazebo. All the while he kept her face in view.

How sweet was her obvious concern.

Except—as he approached, it slowly dawned upon him that it wasn't Sherri's face that he was seeing. It was...

When with horror he guessed whose eyes it was that were gazing into his, panic overtook him and he began to run. As he raced up toward the house away from the gazebo he became the tallest object on the lawn and a bolt of lightening that, he would have thought, would have sought out the copper weathervane instead sought out him and *zap!* felled him to the ground, where he instantly died. ◊

OLD REX
JOY V. SMITH

Joy V. Smith tells us, "It all began when I was a kid and made my own little books, complete with covers. Later I bought an old Royal typewriter with my baby-sitting money. In college (University of Wisconsin—Oshkosh), I spent way too much time writing instead of studying, but I did get published a few times. Since then I've been published in a number of science fiction and other magazines. I also write non-fiction; my interviews have been published in print and online."

She lives in Florida with Xena the warrior puppy.

The two men, their faces blackened, stared down at the dead dog. Its eyes were fixed and glaring, and the foam around its mouth was beginning to dry. "Took him long enough," said the taller of the two men.

The short one shrugged and pulled his hood forward. "He gobbled up the meat quick enough; we'll know to put more poison in the next batch." He moved away from the fence with its crudely cut and jagged edges pushed inward. "Let's get up to the house."

Julie was five, almost six, old enough to be really scared; and she'd been frightened ever since she woke up when the two men pulled her roughly from her bed, even though they'd told her it was just a bad dream and she shouldn't be scared. "Don't want her screaming," the short man had muttered. Now, however, they were carrying her away from the house, away from her father and mother.

She whimpered a couple of times as they moved furtively away from the house; then she saw old Rex lying by the fence. "Rex," she screamed. "Help me, help me."

The man who was carrying her slapped her face. It was not much of a slap—for him. But Julie, even more terrified, screamed again and cried, "Bite them, Rex, bite them." They were almost to the fence now. The short man pushed on ahead, bending the fence outward.

The tall man turned sideways to slip through the opening. He didn't see the dog stagger to his feet and lunge forward, but he felt the cold sharpness of the teeth as they closed on his leg. He sprawled forward, letting Julie tumble to the ground. She was up and off like a deer, fleeing towards the house, where lights and shouting people spilled out to meet her. Her father reached her first, gathered her up and took her to safety.

Several hours later, the tall man, his face sponged clean, lay sweating and trembling in a hospital bed. Outside his door, two policemen spoke briefly. "You won't have any trouble with him, Jack. They've cut off his leg. The doctor said the poison from the dog got into the wound somehow."

The younger cop paused before settling into the chair by the doorway for his shift. "Strange that, wasn't it?" he asked in a puzzled voice. "Rigor mortis had set in so fast they had trouble getting the dog's teeth out of his leg."

The older cop shrugged. "You see some strange things in our line of work," he said philosophically. He added, in a tone that indicated a sudden desire to get his own teeth into someone, "Pity the other one got away. The little girl said there were two bad men."

Jack nodded. He studied his long, brown fingers thoughtfully. "I'd sure like to get my hands on him. Pity the old dog's dead. I bet he'd have tracked him down."

Not quite a week later, Edward Brenner was standing beside Rex's grave when his brother arrived. He smiled, stepped forward, and hugged him tightly for a moment before speaking. "It's good to have you back, Tim. I suppose you know what happened."

"Donna saved all the papers. I read them before I went to bed last night. I got back so late, there was no way I was going to wake you up in the middle of the night—not now."

His brother shuddered. "Thank you for that. It'll take a while to get over waking in the night, panicky, looking for Julie..."

"How is she?" Tim asked uneasily. "She was always such an outgoing, happy kid."

"She still is," her father said with heartfelt gratitude. He gestured to the pansies lying on the grave. "Those are hers. She brings him flowers every day and talks to him."

Tim stared at the grave a few moments before saying, "From the papers I got the impression that some things about the whole situation were a bit strange, or was that just some reporter trying to make it into the tabloids? You know— 'D.A.'s daughter kidnapped for revenge. Daughter's dog comes back from grave to save her.'"

"No," his brother said softly, "the kidnapper said that the dog was dead. He said it over and over until they put him under; the doctor still doesn't understand why his leg was so badly infected. The whole question of rigor mortis is so uncertain anyway, it was just dropped." He looked down at the grave and said harshly, "I'm sorry Rex didn't give him rabies."

Tim glanced at his brother uncertainly. "He had his shots though, didn't he?" he asked cautiously.

Ed looked into the distance with an ice-cold smile. "Rex wouldn't know that," he said. "Like he didn't know he was dead."

Three days later Ed was in his study, working on the scrapbook he'd started. He looked up and smiled when Tim entered the room. "Thanks for coming over," he said. "I wanted you to see this. Maybe you already saw it in the paper."

Tim moved over to stand behind his brother. He read aloud the clipping that his brother had just pasted in the scrapbook. "'Police say fingerprints of dead man found in the shrubbery at Brookside Park match those found in the bedroom of little Julie Brenner. Eyewitness Peter Bryon, who'd been in the park two days earlier collecting aluminum cans, identified the body as the same man he'd seen attacked by what appeared to be a rabid dog. 'It was a black and brown Shepherd cross I think, and it was foaming at the mouth. It ran up to this man, and he started screaming when he seen it coming. I hadn't even noticed him till then—the man that is. Well, there were these little kids around, and I was afraid it would get them after it stopped chewing on the man, so I went towards it swinging my bag—it was pretty full—and I figured I could use it as a shield if I had to. It came up to me—and I swear its eyes were glowing—but it only sniffed me, then backed off. I looked away for a second—some kid's mom was commencing to holler—and it was gone. Must have gone into the bushes. The man was gone too. I figured he'd run off to the hospital. I didn't think much about it till the police couldn't find man or dog. No. No, ma'm, I'm not no hero. I just wanted to save those kids.'"

"That sounds like old Rex, doesn't it?" asked Ed. His fingers, busy smoothing out the clipping, trembled slightly.

"Lord, yes," Tim breathed. "He heard what you said." He sat down heavily in the nearest chair. "Did you mean him to?"

"Yes, I did. I'm not sorry—not really. I wonder, though, do you think I'm crazy, Tim, obsessed...?"

Tim looked steadily at his brother and shook his head. "No. They hurt you and scared you when they took Julie. If it had only been you, you wouldn't have reacted so violently."

Ed smiled slightly. "I'm thinking of giving this scrapbook to Julie—when she's older, of course, and telling her that if she's ever in trouble to call Rex with all her might. Now, what do you think?"

"I think she'd be better off if you taught her how to protect herself," Tim said sharply. "You can't expect Rex to always be there for her."

"Of course," Ed said. "I realize that; but if there's ever a time when she's really desperate..."

Tim sighed. "I guess I'd do it." He thought for a moment; he had a vague idea of leading his older brother onto a safer path. "You got Rex at the pound, didn't you?"

Ed leaned back in his old wooden desk chair and relaxed a bit. "Yes," he told Tim, remembering. "He was a stray—not much to look at. He was already at the leggy, awkward stage, but he looked at me with eyes that said— 'Get me out of here, and I will serve you faithfully all my life.' All my life," Ed repeated.

"And beyond," Tim said. He hadn't meant to. He thought he'd checked his tongue, but it popped out.

Ed stood up suddenly and shoved his chair back. "I'm going to the pound this afternoon with Julie. She's going to choose a puppy." He looked at Tim. "I don't expect it to be like Rex, of course. But a kid needs a dog—one she can play with; and I'd feel a little safer too. Also, if I can save one dog—the way Rex saved Julie, I'd feel better... Maybe you'd like to come along."

"Yeah," Tim said. "I think maybe I'll save one too. Like you said, it won't be like Rex, but a dog is a good thing to have around the house, especially when I'm off traveling. I never worried about it before—not here. Now, though..."

"Yes, now though," Ed repeated bitterly. He paused, took a deep breath. "By the way," he said, more calmly, "this morning the gardener told me Rex's grave had been torn up a bit—not a big hole or anything—only scratched up a bit. He asked if I wanted him to put some more dirt on it and pack it down harder. I said no. I said just rake it smooth and leave it. He was relieved, I think."

Tim nodded in agreement. "Not that more dirt would stop him, but why make it harder for the old boy." He wondered if his brother was thinking, as he was, of the man in the hospital. ◇

IN THE HEAT OF THE DAY
MARIA POLLACK

Maria Pollack is an Assistant Professor of English at Hudson Valley Community College. Her short fiction has been published in The Detroit Jewish News, The Little Magazine, The Loyalhanna Review, Quantum Tao, Wings, *and* Urban Desires, *a Web-based magazine. She lives in upstate New York.*

There is always a woman's voice in the wind—sometimes singing, sometimes whispering, sometimes calling, but, in winter storms, always crying.

She walks the perimeter of the island. My husband claims she does not exist, that I just have an overactive imagination. He just doesn't realize she hides herself from him. Why would she want to show herself to any man after what happened?

When it gets hot in the afternoon and I can no longer stand to shift through the same old sheet music and play the same old tunes on the piano, I go down to the ocean. As I cross the field, I turn and look back at the light. From high up on the scaffolding, my husband waves to me, and I return the gesture. He has his shirt off, and his chest and stomach—turned golden from the long days of scraping and painting in the hot July sun—glisten with sweat.

As I turn away from him, I touch my rounded stomach. I think of all the nights last winter when he rose above me, and I wrapped my legs around him. In the half-darkness of the cold white moonlight, I watched his dark eyes and noticed his half smile as I opened myself up to him. Together, we rocked slowly, like two boats on a sleepy sea.

The baby will be coming soon, and I miss my mother and sister more than ever.

From among the rocks, I gather an abundance of saltspray roses. They have huge magenta blossoms, vibrant yellow centers, and thick, snaky stems. I bring them up to the house and put them in vases which I fill to the brim with fresh water. But, I know in this heat that by tomorrow they will be wilted, their petals shriveled and blackened.

I can't remember it ever being so oppressive, even when I lived in the city.

Perhaps, Evelyn won't come to the window tonight. To appease her, I left some apples at her grave. I know she's hungry. Her eyes, huge like twin black tidal pools, are always staring. Endlessly staring. But what can I give her?

They say she played the piano every night, waiting and trying not to listen to the screaming November wind. It was the storms which kept her husband away. She tended the light. There was no more flour, no more salt pork.

The baby in her womb stopped moving. She wondered if her husband had been lost, if he had drowned beneath the icy cold waves. Who would come to claim her?

Her mother had long been in her grave, and Evelyn had never had any sisters or brothers. There had only been her father, but she had been glad to be rid of him.

At night, sometimes, he'd come home drunk and push open her bedroom door. When he put his heavy, stinking hand over her mouth, he told her she owed him. It was because of her his life was cursed, his beloved wife dead now sixteen years. But she knew differently. She'd heard the stories about how he'd terrorized her, how he'd pushed her down the back staircase bringing on Evelyn's birth, how her mother was better off dead.

Jack was handsome, shy, gentle. He brought her books, sheet music, and sweets. He told her it would be a lonely life, and she told him she didn't care, for, at least, it would be a life.

When he returned, Jack found her—dressed, as if for her bridal night, in a simple white cotton gown—in their bed. At first, he thought she was sleeping, she looked so peaceful, her skin so smooth, so radiant, almost luminescent like the phosphorescence of the sea. But, her hands, her cheeks, her lips were cold. After he buried her, he went back to the mainland and soon another couple came to the lighthouse.

They told us stories of a woman singing, the sudden scent of roses in an upstairs bedroom even in the middle of winter, and a mysterious light down among the rocks. On that warm June evening, just three days after our wedding, we laughed at the stories. But that was over a year ago. That was all before I first heard Evelyn's singing.

The heat grows unbearable in the afternoon. I carry a basin of cold water up to our room. I take my clothes off and tie my hair back. I wash myself slowly, methodically and notice, in the mirror which hangs above the dresser, all the changes in my face and body. My eyes have dark circles beneath them, and although my shoulders are still pale and white, my breasts have become dun-colored. They are heavy and swollen.

When I finish, I lie beneath a cool, freshly laundered sheet and try to sleep. With night comes lightening and rain. David checks on me. I tell him I'm fine. He asks if I want supper, and I say I just want to sleep. He quietly closes the bedroom door behind him when he leaves.

I'm awakened by her voice. She's singing a lullaby, one my mother used to sing to me and my sister about a babe, fast asleep, in his cradle that has washed out to sea. She stands over my bed and places her icy hand against my mouth. My lungs burn. Cool tears stream down my cheeks. I am drowning. I am drowning. I am lost forever in a cold, black sea.

"Push!" David screams. "Push!"

We name him Joshua, after David's father. I dress him in his Christening gown and hold him to my breast. I have nothing to give. David comes and takes him from me.

"He's hungry," I say, although my baby no longer cries, not even making the slightest mewling like a newborn kitten.

David just stares at me.

He takes me to the small grave he's dug on the hillside, but I won't look at the cross he's made or the flowers he's picked. Instead, I ask him, "Why is she here?"

That night I begin to play on the piano the same song my mother sang to me when I was a child. It's called Suo-Gan, an ancient Welsh lullaby. The melody drifts across the black rocking water, far out to sea.

David begs me to stop. He forbids me to play. He says I am driving him crazy, but it's the only way I can still my baby's crying. We go on like this, endlessly as the waves.

In the heat of the day, with the sun blazing overhead, he stands beside me. His hair is matted and his eyes are wide open. He lifts the axe high above his head, and I hear the splinter of wood, the twanging of strings, the crack of keys. Afterwards, there is silence. David just stares at me as if he doesn't recognize me. Sweat drips down his face.

This time, when he lifts the blade high above his head, I raise my arms to shield my face, but that's when I hear her singing. I look up and she has my baby in her arms. She moves towards me. It's as if she wants me to take the child from her. I reach out for him, to put him to my breast, to rock him forever to sleep. ◊

WAITING FOR MR. ELDREDGE
CHARLES DANZOLL

After a long career at Cigna (formerly Connecticut General Life Insurance Company), Charles Danzoll retired with his wife to Grantham, New Hampshire. He is the author of another published work, a history of his fraternity chapter at Wesleyan University.

Who am I? Why call me Christopher. Will you listen to my story? Some years ago, when I was a boy of twelve, my mother and father took me and my younger brother, Gregg, to the coastline of Maine for the summer.

We two boys had a lot of fun that summer. Picture us in your mind jumping over the giant rounded rocks tumbled down by the sea, the sun warm on our bare shoulders; picture us exploring the small, lonely islands that stand within easy rowing distance from the shore, or building forts made of logs and cut branches in the woods, or at night, just before bedtime, bending over a campfire down by the water, the two of us trying to keep warm in the sudden cold blowing off the sea, the sky above us alive with stars from horizon to horizon. Gregg and I were close to nature then: the seagulls, small land animals, and bright wildflowers down by the road all seemed to accept our presence in their world.

Yes, we had a lot of fun that summer... except perhaps for one night I'm going to tell you about this evening. Things happened during that night which disturb me even now, as an adult, to remember and so I don't tell this story very often, and when I do, it's only to children and special grownups: people like yourselves who don't scare very easily, but who at the same time are tuned-in to the dark and cold undersides of life, to the world of things unseen and unheard: to ghosts who move and sometimes murder in the night.

It began harmlessly enough: at the public dock of Camden, Maine, on a sunny afternoon in August. My parents had chartered a large white sailboat to take the four of us on an overnight cruise down the coast. The plan was to thread our way south by ship's engine past the spruce-wooded islands that confront the rocky coves of the Maine coastline, and meander along until we reached the town of Wiscasset the next day. There, we were to meet friends of my parents, whose name I've forgotten, and stay with them awhile.

Our sailboat had its own floating wooden dock. It connected to the town's large concrete pier which curved around the three sides of Camden's pretty little harbor. I remember standing on the rough, sunbaked boards of the dock and looking up at the tall, twin masts of the sailboat. It was a very active scene: the harbor was crowded with sail and power boats of every size and description, gaily riding at anchor under the hot sun, and the waterfront thronged with the usual mix of people one meets in that kind of vacation setting: family groups, students, older couples, kids on the loose, and the occasional lone-wolf person, with something queer about his or her look or dress, who didn't seem to fit into any place in life. But I ignored all this activity, having eyes only for the sailboat we were just about to board. It was to be my first time aboard such a craft, and I was very excited, as any twelve-year-old would be. You've probably seen large sailboats like this one, in harbors and marinas along any coast: the long, gracefully curved hull, bright white in the sun; the dark polished wood of the cabins; the tall masts pointing thin and straight into the air: all in all, a graceful thing, grave and gay at the same time, looking beautifully at home on the water.

A friendly voice broke through my thoughts: "Hello there. How 'bout saying Hi to your Captain?"

I looked the man over; he seemed friendly enough. "Hi," I said, shaking his outstretched hand. "My name is Christopher. I really like your boat. Is it very new?"

The Captain nodded, but didn't answer. He waited for me to say something more. He wore khaki work clothes, had a knife in a leather sheaf tied to his belt, and sported a Red Sox baseball hat which was cocked over one ear.

Then I knew what I wanted to ask him about. The day before, my father had read Gregg and me an exciting story about something that had happened on an island nearby. "Do you know anything about an island called Dark Island?"

"Dark Island?" repeated the Captain. "What about it?"

"Are we going near it tonight...on our cruise?"

"Maybe...depends on things..."

"What things?"

"Oh, just certain things," the Captain said. "What did you hear about Dark Island?"

"Well," I said, "my father took me and my brother Gregg to a museum here yesterday, and we saw a lot of things, stuff about the sea, and things like that. My father read us a story from an old yellow newspaper behind glass on the wall. It was about a murder on a place called Dark Island. Something about an old lobsterman who got his throat cut from *ear to ear*...a long time ago."

"Don't remember anything like that ever happening around here," said the Captain. "Best to let such things be and not disturb yourself."

I wasn't happy with his answers; was he holding something back? "You didn't answer my question," I began...

"Easy there, my friend," the Captain interrupted. He was looking over my shoulder.

A man was walking down the pier toward us and our boat. He was alone. There wasn't anything strange about him. But as I looked at the unknown man coming toward us with a steady tread, for a long moment nothing else seemed to move under that hot afternoon sun. Finally, in a voice that sounded strangely far away and disconnected, the Captain broke the sun-struck silence: "Well, I wasn't expecting *him* today." There was a grim smile on his face. He touched me on the arm. "We might have to go to Dark Island after all, tonight." He paused. "But I'm not sure that you'll like it there."

The next thing I remember we were on the sailboat. Its engine was running quietly and we were slipping slowly out of Camden harbor. My parents were in the forward cabin, having a late afternoon drink. Gregg and I stood together outside on the deck. All of a sudden, Gregg jumped up on top of the railing, grabbed an overhanging line and swung out over the water. With a big grin on his face, he stretched his arms and legs so that his body made the shape of an "x" as he curved through the air and came back toward the boat. In no time at all, Gregg was on the deck beside me again.

"What'd you do that for?" I asked, not really surprised. Gregg was seven to my twelve, and was capable of doing anything, good or bad, under the sun. He laughed: "I just felt like being an "x," that's all. What's wrong with that?" Picture in your mind a little boy with blond hair, hard body and broad shoulders, with the face of a determined angel, and you've got Gregg. In contrast, people tell me I was dark, tall and quiet: nervous and quick like a deer, with pondering features.

"What's the matter, Christopher?" said Gregg. "Why don't you talk to me?"

"I'm just thinking, Gregg. About nothing special."

But that wasn't really true. I was thinking about Dark Island and the man whose throat had been cut from ear-to-ear. In the harbor the flock of white boats were gaily riding at anchor under the late afternoon sun, but I really didn't notice them. I remembered what my father said in the museum the day before.

"...There were two brothers named Eldredge: old men, lobstermen, living alone on Dark Island many years ago. They kept to themselves. Though of an old village family, no one knew them anymore. One day, another lobsterman was tending his pots in the channel near the island. He happened to look over and saw the two brothers fighting outside their cabin. They were hitting each other with their fists, holding nothing back. Being a strong young man and not afraid of anything, the other lobsterman quickly rowed over to the island, clambered up the rocks and ran through the trees to stop the fight. But he was too late. In the meantime, the struggle had moved inside the cabin, and when the young man ran in, he found one of the brothers lying on his back in a bloodstained bed, not quite dead. His throat was cut from ear to ear; his arms were outstretched in the air; his head strained off of the reddened pillow. He tried to say something, but all the young man could hear through that ripped throat was the sound, '*Crch—crcccch...crch—crcccch.*' Then the old man sank back dead on the bloody sheets, and the lobsterman charged out of the cabin to find the brother.

"From the other side of the island he could hear the sound of cursing and shouting; words, phrases floated back: angry jumbles of sound... 'Kill... leave me in peace... kill... I'll kill anyone who follows me... kill.' Then the shouting suddenly stopped as if choked off, and the young man began to search the island, moving slowly back and forth, checking out each place a man might hide. But he found no one."

Mr. Eldredge had vanished, like a ghost, and I remembered what my father had said to me, with a laugh, as he finished telling me the story. "The murderer disappeared into thin air—think of that, Christopher—and his body was never found. Maybe he's out there yet, old Mr. Eldredge; somewhere nearby in the mists of the sea, waiting to kill anyone who tries to catch him..."

The newspaper article was accompanied by a photograph of the brothers, taken shortly before the murder: two big grey-bearded men standing in their black slickers outside their cabin on Dark Island. One man leaned heavily on the longest axe I've ever seen; the other, the one who was murdered, I think, held by his side what looked like an old Civil War cavalry saber. Both men stared at the camera with hard angry eyes, as if blaming the innocent viewer for their lives of poverty, hard work and loneliness: the long cold winters, just the two of them together; the dulling round of catching the bait, minding the traps, mending the gear, fixing the boat... just the two of them alone.

I leaned over the rail, looking at really nothing. The water had changed to a duller color in the late afternoon light. The only sound was the steady plank-plank of the boat's engine. We were slipping through a narrow channel between two islands close together. These large rounded masses of ledge and tumbled rock, topped by thick green stands of spruce trees, were stolidly silent except for the cries of gulls: a world somehow outside of the lives of men.

We passed within twenty feet of an old lobster boat which was tilted upon its side against a rock on one of the islands. The wood was grey, worn smooth by the sea wind. The thick curving braces lay exposed, giving the thing the structural, stripped-down look of a skeleton. A bright green clump of grass grew through one of the holes in the bottom. Gregg put his hand in mine; a light mist had blown up without warning and over the bow of our sailboat I could see a pair of lobster-pots beyond the islands, bobbing up and down, disappearing in the mist and then appearing again. I shivered, though it wasn't cold. To me, this small quiet world of sea, sky and islands still belonged more to the murderer, Mr. Eldredge, than it did to Gregg and me.

I thought of the old lobsterman: a grey ghost in his slicker and rubber boots, rowing his boat without a sound in the night, endlessly on watch for his pursuers: a ghost with sharp knife at the ready, keeping his boat close to the sheltering islands: appearing, then disappearing, then appearing again in the mists that boil up from the sea.

"Hey, Christopher," Gregg cried. "Who's that guy over there?" Gregg was talking in that rough, pretend-tough tone of his. "What's he doing on our boat?"

Gregg was pointing forward, toward the area behind the cabin. No one had been there before, but a man stood there now. He wasn't the Captain; the Captain was inside. This was a different man. I wasn't absolutely sure then, but he looked like the man on the dock, at Camden: the man who had approached us alone, with steady tread, in that blinding sunstruck moment, hours ago.

Gregg ambled over to him, his hands jammed into the pockets of his short pants, like a little tough guy.

"How did you get here?" Gregg asked. "I didn't see you come on our boat. This boat belongs just to us."

"Oh, I'm a special friend of the Captain's," the man said in a good-humored, confiding way.

"But that doesn't answer my question..."

"Well," the man laughed, "how did *you* get here? I didn't

see *you* come on board. But here you are, real as can be. So I must be real, too. Right?"

Gregg looked the man over, then nodded. "Yeah, you're real, I can tell *that*."

The man leaned down and touched Gregg on the shoulder. Gregg didn't seem to mind. "How old are you?"

"Seven, almost eight." A pause, then: "How old are *you*?"

The man straightened up. "A little older than seven, almost eight. What's your name?"

"Gregg. This is my brother, Christopher."

The man held up the palm of his hand to me in silent salute. Then, back to Gregg: "You know, Gregg, whether you know it or not, you're beginning to grow away from something very special and precious, so try and grow away from it as slowly as you can."

"What's that?" I popped in, feeling a little left out.

He turned to me, a tall man with a sharp face, clean shaven and tanned: an image of high cheek bones, staring eyes that seemed to look beyond you. I found myself wondering if he had a friend in the world.

He pointed to something resting on the deck, next to his feet. Somehow, I hadn't noticed it before, but now there was an old heavy sea chest on the deck. Battered and discolored, it looked as if it had accompanied its owner on a hundred long voyages on all the five great oceans of the world. But the chest still appeared strong and tight. Great bands of brass encircled it, and there was a big round brass lock in the clasp.

"Supposing I asked you, Gregg, to believe in something you couldn't see or touch or hear, but which even so was grand and marvelous and beautiful. Do you think you could believe in it?"

Gregg looked up at him, a sly wondering smile on his face; he nodded "yes."

"Then guess what's inside this chest."

"Can I look inside?"

"No."

"Why?"

"It's a special chest," the man said. "It can't be opened by anyone in this world. Now what's your guess?"

Gregg knelt down beside the chest and ran his fingers over the scarred leather and great brass bands. On one side, he found the faint outline of a great eagle—a fierce lordly image—which had been embossed in gold into the leather covering. He ran his finger over the tensed wings and then tugged mightily at the lock.

"I think," Gregg finally said, "that something marvelous and strange is inside here."

The man nodded, smiling. Then he turned to me. "What about you, Christopher? What do you think is in the chest?"

I touched it, too. In fact, with a quick surge of strength I tried to move it; but the chest seemed bolted to the deck. I couldn't budge it. "You're not going to give me any hints?"

"So you're old enough to need *hints*," the man replied. "How old *are* you."

I gave way to a rising anger. "Twelve," I shouted. "Almost thirteen. Anyway, I don't think there's *anything* in that chest. I bet it's empty."

The man smiled again. "Well, that's an answer, too." He turned toward the water and shivered a little. "B-r-r-r. It's getting chilly." He paused. "The shadows have lengthened, the busy world is hushed, and the evening's come..." He paused again. "I had forgotten how chilly summer evenings in Maine can be, after the sun goes down."

"Where do you live?" asked Gregg.

"Where do *I* live? Oh, I don't really have a home."

He made his answer sound as if it were the most natural answer in the world. Then, seeing Gregg's concerned look, he said lightly, "Don't worry, it's all right. Some people don't need homes."

Gregg looked him over, at first saying nothing. Then: "If you say so. Now I have another question for you: What's your name?"

"What's my name?" the man repeated, smiling. "Orlando. You may call me Orlando."

"Orlando what?"

"Just Orlando," the man said. "Nothing more, nothing less."

At that, the man called Orlando looked inquiringly at me and, determined to press him to get the answers I believed I was entitled to, I said, "Why *are* you on our boat?"

He barked out a laugh. A seagull flying by veered away at the sound, as if it had been a gunshot. I was sorry I asked the question. Orlando looked now like the eagle on his chest—lordly, fierce. He gestured over the water. "Because your course takes me to where I must be tonight. That island over there."

It was an island like many we had come upon and left in our wake that summer afternoon. There was nothing strange about it. It was small by Maine-island standards. Looking at it, sizing the place up, I guessed you could probably pick your way around the island's rocky shore in half an hour. Above the ledges and rocks at the shoreline, there rose the familiar masses of dark green spruce trees, so tightly packed you wondered how anything—man or beast—could force its way through.

A headland of great oddly shaped boulders fronted the island and took the full force of the sea. Rank upon rank, the waves boiled up and crashed against the rocks, sending thin jets of water high in the air, and making underneath a low roaring sound: a rhythmic washing turbulence that seemed timeless and unceasing. I followed the lifting spray with my eyes and saw against the darkening sky a lone seagull slowly circling over the headland, larger than normal, with great white wings. Behind the headland there was a clearing, backed by long lines of dark spruce. In the clearing I could just make out the weathered grey shape of an old cabin. Even from this distance, the place had an air of longtime emptiness. There was no glass in the windows, the door hung open, and part of the roof had fallen in.

"They call this place Dark Island," Orlando said softly. "The Captain will be anchoring here awhile tonight."

The plunk-plunk of the engines suddenly stopped. Our boat cut noiselessly through the water. I gripped the rail with both hands, heart beating fast. We were close to the island now: a five-minute row. The anchor chain clattered through the bow hole and slipped into the water. Our boat was tugged to a stop. I half-closed my eyes and tried to blot out everything in sight except the island. I focused my whole being on the dark headland, on the old cabin.

Time passed. I thought I heard Orlando say, " ...I have an appointment here, Christopher; I have an appointment here tonight... on Dark Island. It's a long story... Will you listen to my story? Will you and Gregg come with me tonight?... We will meet Mr. Eldredge... Will you and Gregg come with me tonight, will you listen to my story?"

My eyes were closed all the way now, and I could feel the cold polished wood of the deck rail press against my cheek, and my breathing was slow and regular like the movements of the sea. Time passed, and the evening fell over the sea, and I dreamt of two men standing in their slickers for the photographer long ago; one holding an axe, the other a cavalry saber. I dreamt of them fighting each other in the clearing; then, in the cabin, tearing at each other with knives, and then of one man dying in a blood-soaked bed, mouthing "C-cch-h... C-ccccc-c-c-h..." over and over again, while his brother ran through the woods yelling "... kill... kill... kill."

I dreamt of this man, Mr. Eldredge, the murderer, abroad on

the sea, after the evening fell, poling his lobster boat past the islands, muttering to himself and watching and waiting, knife at the ready in the darkness. And then I dreamt of another man, the man called Orlando—fierce, too, and lordly like an eagle, with his sea chest and smiling, quiet manner and strange sayings—a man who also waited, but without movement and in grave dark silence.

"Careful now," Orlando whispered. "No talking."

It was later that night. Gregg and I huddled together on the rear seat of the sailboat's dinghy. Orlando sat facing us on the middle seat, leaning into each stroke of the oars. The oarlocks grated noisily when he pulled, and the boat seemed to fly over the moonlit water. Orlando wore a long black robe, and I couldn't see his face because of the hood that shadowed his features.

"We're getting closer," he said. "Be ready."

I looked over his shoulder and saw in front of us the headland of Dark Island. The large smooth rocks were colored dirty yellow in the moonlight, and I could hear the steady wash of the waves as they broke against the shore. Behind us our sailboat rode at anchor: dark except for small red and green pilot lights fore and aft.

Gregg shivered against me. "Golly, Christopher, I'm cold."

I shivered, too, but not just from the wind blowing off from the dark moving water. Between us and Orlando rested his sea chest on the wide bottom of the boat.

"You two carry the chest," he whispered, as the bow of our dinghy made contact with the sand.

"It's too heavy," I said.

"You can do it if you try," Orlando answered.

We jumped out of the dinghy and helped pull it up the beach; the small boat, I noticed, didn't have a name—only three fading letters painted on the white stern board: *M C A.*

Orlando reached under his robe and pulled out a long wooden torch which he suddenly wooshed into flames at the end. He raised the torch high over his hooded head and waved it toward a path that cut up the headland to the clearing on top. In his dark flowing robes, with long arm extended, his figure bathed in vibrating light, Orlando looked like some kind of weird angel of the night.

Gregg and I picked up the chest: my brother in front, me behind. Orlando was right; it wasn't heavy now. We followed him across the little beach, nestled in between large rounded rocks, and picked our way up the path. The light from his torch made it fairly easy for us to trudge around the rocks, but at one point—without warning—Gregg dropped the chest as something very fast whizzed by our ears in the night.

"The *gull*," cried Gregg. "She's attacking us."

I was shaking all over—the thing had come so close: a hissing blur of speed from out of, it seemed, the black mysterious heart of nature itself. I followed the great seagull as it completed its pass and curved around through the night to find its place high up in the sky, behind us again. There, so white in the moonlight, it hung for a long moment against the darkness, riding high above us without moving, as if gathering its forces for another desperate attack.

Just as the seagull began its silent descent, curving down towards us again, Orlando bellowed out a horrible sound—"Arggggggggggh"—and waved his flaming torch at the bird one time only. As if shot, the great bird slid away from us through the air, away from the island and over the water again, and over our sailboat riding at anchor in the channel, to disappear in darkness over an island on the other side.

"I warned you boys," Orlando said firmly. "This will not be an easy night... for anyone on this island. Now pick up the chest.

We don't want to be late for our appointment, do we?"

Inside the cabin there was a dark, closed-up smell. It seemed to seep from deep within the old floor boards and grey walls, and reminded me of old cellars, empty prisons, and graveyards in the rain. Now Orlando's torch flared, sputtered, almost going out at one point, as if suddenly starved for air in that gloomy room. Gregg's hand slipped into mine; the three of us looked around the cabin without saying anything. For the first time, I sensed in Orlando a hesitancy, perhaps even a fear; he who before had been fierce and lordly like an eagle, who in his mystery conveyed to the two of us a strength and a power that was beyond our young knowing.

Through the dusty gloom I could see a great stone fireplace taking up one whole side of the room. At various intervals in the massive stone front there were shadowed square openings of different sizes—two large holes near the floor (for firewood, I guessed) and other smaller holes higher up that looked like cooking or warming ovens. Directly across the room from the fireplace I could make out what had once been an eating area. Behind a small round table and chairs, there was a kitchen sink built into a rough counter against the wall. On top of the counter rested a small hand pump for water; its spout hung over the sink. Over the counter I could see a cupboard that still had plates, pans, and glasses on its dusty shelves.

A sofa sagged by itself in the middle of the room. Its upholstery was eaten away in places and some springs showed through the dusty cloth. On the side between the fireplace and the eating area, a door with several missing boards led to the only other room in the cabin. The door hung ajar, disclosing only dark shapes and shadows in what had once probably been the bedroom. On the other side of the big room, opposite the bedroom and next to the front door, there was a row of large wooden pegs and an adjoining shelf that still held some articles.

I could see two oars, something that looked like a harpoon, and a long-handled axe and cavalry sword. Next to the sword, there was mounted the head of a stuffed deer.

"Hey, this sure is a creepy place," Gregg whispered hoarsely. "I don't like it much in here. Want to play outside?"

I made a move to go with him, but Orlando said, "A fire in that fireplace will warm things up. There's kindling and wood in the corner. Which one of you is good at making fires?"

"*Me*," said Gregg.

"*Me*," I said.

"Go to it then, both of you. We may have to wait here awhile."

"For who?" I asked, glancing at the front door, which creaked slowly back and forth.

"Why, you know who, Christopher. I told you earlier, on the boat." Orlando's tone was quiet, neutral; but I sensed nervousness running behind his words. "We're waiting for Mr. Eldredge. The man who lived in this house and murdered his brother here, in that bedroom, a long time ago. We're waiting for Mr. Eldredge tonight."

At these words, I felt cold all over. I waited for him to say something more. But Orlando looked away. Gregg started to gather up the firewood, humming happily to himself as if this kind of experience happened to him all the time. I joined him in the work, but with beating heart.

Soon, with a fire blazing in the great stone hearth, the room seemed less threatening and strange. Gregg and I sat on the floor in front of the fire, with our backs against the sea chest. Orlando stood to one side, leaning silently against the mantle. His motionless robed figure seemed to match the mood of the place. The torch, stuck into the frame of the old sofa in the middle of the room, sputtered in the darkness beyond the firelight. Above the torch there was a big hole in the roof and, framed inside the round jagged edges of broken shingle, I could see a patch of blue-black night sky and a maze of stars sprinkled over it far above: cold white pinpricks of light, impossibly far away from Gregg and me on Dark Island.

"...And so I'm going to leave you boys alone for a while," Orlando was saying. "Mr. Eldredge won't be here until later on. But if he should come while I'm away, tell him that the man called Orlando says to wait for him. He'll do that, for we have an appointment and he and I know each other from another time and place."

"How?" I asked.

Orlando was almost out the front door. He turned toward us. "Don't you know yet, Christopher? Mr. Eldredge belongs to the place I come from, to the place he and I must return to." Orlando's voice dropped; his hooded figure, still confronting me, seemed to lose its substance. "In a way he and I are like brothers, Christopher; and there's a special place, far from here, for men like Mr. Eldredge and myself... *who have murdered other men.*"

"You, too," I whispered. "You're a murderer, too?"

But the man called Orlando was gone. The front door creaked a little. There was no other sound.

Gregg and I looked at each other. Our friend, Orlando, a murderer? Who did he kill? Why did he do it? What did he want from us? When was he coming back? And what about Mr. Eldredge, who was on his way here now? What would become of us?

"Don't worry, Christopher," whispered Gregg. "Everything will be all right. *I'll protect you.*"

"Fat chance you will," I whispered back.

Some time passed. We two must have fallen asleep by the fire. The next thing I knew, only coals glowed in the hearth. My eyes were heavy from sleep. Gregg snored quietly away, his arms flung over the chest.

I looked around. Something moved by the front door. He came in without a sound. At first, in the gloom of the room, I thought he was just another part of the darkness, a blacker shadow, but—no—the shape emerging from the doorway was that of a man, a tall man with great shoulders, much older and bigger than our friend. This one had a beard and leaned on a heavy walking stick.

I grabbed Gregg and pulled him with me around the chest and over to behind the sofa in the middle of the room. Gregg was awake now and began to struggle against me. I put my hand over his mouth so that he couldn't say anything and pointed towards the man.

"It's *him*," I whispered. "Mr. Eldredge."

Gregg nodded. "I know," he calmly said.

We peeped out at him over the top of the sofa. With an old man's uncertainty, Mr. Eldredge stepped heavily across the room. He paused at the kitchen sink, his broad back toward us. I could hear the sound of the water pump handle being worked several times. No water gushed up. He turned again, facing the room and lifting one arm straight out. It pointed towards us.

"There are presences in this room," he said, in a low rumbling voice. "I can feel you in the darkness. Two little presences, two little *ghosts*." Then, in a rising voice, the words tumbling over one another: "Who are you? Me and my brother when we were both young? Leave me alone. Leave me alone, whoever you are. Or I will kill you." His arm fell to his side. With his other arm he lunged and swung his walking stick over our heads—I could hear the whirring sound as the stick sliced through the air.

Gregg and I scattered towards the fireplace behind us. Mr. Eldredge advanced across the room with heavy deliberate tread. He stumbled over the sofa and, in the darkness, suddenly disappeared from my view.

I crouched behind the sea chest. "Gregg," I whispered. There was no answer. "Gregg."

Then a huge hand came out of the darkness and gave me a terrific blow on the shoulder. I rolled across the floor, trying to get out of Mr. Eldredge's way. The room was alive with the sound of his heavy breathing, with the smell of the salt air from his clothing. I couldn't see him in the darkness. The walking stick hissed through the air: once, several times, the last time right over my head. I stayed where I was behind the sea chest; in the silence, I could feel his presence towering over me, almost see his face with its bristling white beard and hard, angry eyes looking down at me. Then, there was an emptiness in the air, almost a black hole, if you can imagine that; strangely, after being so close, Mr. Eldredge turned away. Through the blackness I could hear his footsteps receding toward the kitchen area across the room.

"Christopher," my brother softly said. "Over here, by the fireplace." I crawled toward the sound of Gregg's voice. His hand came out of the darkness and pulled me into one of the large openings in the stone front of the fireplace for storing wood. We crept around behind some old logs that were stacked in the hole and peered over the top of the pile into the room.

"What's he doing now?" Gregg whispered in my ear.

"He's over by the kitchen cupboard. Oh-oh. He just lit a match." There was a splutter of flame, sharp and small in the blackness; then, the spreading warm light of an oil lamp. "Oh-my-gosh, Gregg. With the light he can find us. We're in trouble now."

"No, *he's* in trouble now." A different voice had spoken, close to us in the room. I jumped, then relaxed. It was the voice of our friend, Orlando. His hooded shape detached itself from the shadows around the front door, and his torch flared in the gloom. He turned and faced Mr. Eldredge, who stared back at him, still holding the oil lamp with a steady hand: a silent unmoving shape which bulked heavily across the room.

"Excuse me for not being here when you arrived," Orlando said to Mr. Eldredge politely. Orlando seemed to be his usual self again; the hesitancy, the fear that I had felt earlier had gone. "I had to go to a private place just now—away from this house of murder—for instructions from the other world as to what to do with you."

Mr. Eldredge shook his head. "Your instructions—whatever they may be—have nothing to do with me."

"Shall we go into the bedroom?" our friend asked softly. "We can talk in there better."

"There's nothing to talk about," Mr. Eldredge responded in his deep rolling tones. "There are reasons for what I did."

Our friend laughed harshly. "There are always reasons for murdering one's own brother." Then, in a commanding voice and with a wave of the torch: "Come with me. You know you have no choice. You and I must return to the other world, to the place where we both belong."

Mr. Eldredge sighed. He started to say something, then turned without a word and went into the other oom, followed by Orlando who closed the door after him.

Immediately, our friend opened the door again and looked out at us. "I almost forgot about you two." With a sudden effort, he smiled at us and drew up his body straight and tall by the bedroom door. "Gregg and Christopher, this night ends for you now. You and I will not meet again. All I ask is that you ponder upon what you have seen and heard, and that some day you will tell the story of this night." He paused, and when he spoke again, it was in another, warmer tone. "I leave to you both my sea chest as a memento of the evening." He raised his hand to us. "Gregg, I salute your faith. Christopher, I salute your courage." His hand dropped. One last image of high cheekbones, staring eyes: a strange presence, fierce and lordly like an eagle. He turned back into the dark bedroom, and the door closed again.

For the next several minutes we crouched in our hidey hole in the wall of the fireplace and listened to the low murmur of the two men's conversation. I could make out only an occasional word. The light from Orlando's torch seeped through the cracks in the bedroom wall, but otherwise our room was dark. By now, even the coals in the fireplace had mostly gone out.

In the other room, without warning, there was a large crash, followed by a shouted curse. The full length of a body hit hard against the wall, and the whole house shook. A heavy blow. A groan. Another heavy blow. Another groan.

"So it's knives again," one of them yelled.

Sounds of furniture being kicked aside, and the frantic shuffling of feet against the floorboards. Another wild yell. I visualized the two of them grappling together in the dim light of the torch, their knives working in and out. The excitement lifted me out of the hidey hole and I ran across the room toward the bedroom door. The most awful human scream I ever heard filled the cabin and the night, stopping me dead in my tracks. I paused, then made it to the door and put my ear against a loose panel.

The scream had subsided into a different sound: "Crch-chcch-crch-crccccch." I heard, knowing without really thinking about it that someone was trying to talk through a throat that had just been slashed by a knife. "Crch-crcccch-crcch." Then silence, no sound at all. I waited, hearing nothing. I put my hand to the door knob, yet feared to open it: what if it was our friend, Orlando, lying dead or dying on a blood-soaked bed? Gregg's hand slipped into mine; together we stood there, facing the bedroom door.

"Let's go in," Gregg said.

I hesitated, then pushed the door open and looked around. What do you think I saw? It just wasn't possible. The room was empty.

There was no sign of the two men. The flickering torch showed an old bed sagging against the wall, a khaki blanket folded neatly at the bottom. Mr. Eldredge's old lamp glowed placidly on top of a small dresser in another dusty corner. The curtains around the only window in the room rustled in the night air.

"Where did they go?" Gregg asked.

I rubbed my eyes. Had it all been just a dream? I took the oil lamp and knelt on the floor and caused the light to shine on the dusty floorboards. Except for our own, there were no other footprints, not to mention signs of the struggle we had listened to, like blood or an abandoned knife. Underneath the opened window, thick dust lay on the wide floorboards undisturbed.

"Where did they go?" Gregg asked again.

"I don't know."

"Where's Orlando?"

"Orlando's gone," I said.

"Were they really in this room?"

"Look at the oil lamp and torch," I said. "Who else brought them here?"

"You're right," Gregg said. "They must have been in this room." He went to the window and looked up at the night sky. "Hey, Christopher. I think I see the two of them flying through the air, far, far away."

I joined him at the window and followed his pointing finger. I thought I saw the shapes of two men floating upwards in the heavens, hand-in-hand, but lost them in all the stars before I could be sure.

Shortly afterward, Gregg and I left the cabin. After putting out the torch and lamp, there was nothing left for us to do in there. The cabin was empty once more—just an old ruin left to decay to nothing on an island empty of people as well.

We carried the sea chest down the path to the beach. It was not as dark now. In fact, the sun was rising out of the sea far to the east of us. There was a new fresh salty flavor to the air. The gulls were making their cawing sounds again. Everywhere else there was silence, except for the low unceasing wash of the sea as it rushed against the ledges and the rocks in an incoming tide. We decided to wait on the beach for the tide to come up a little. This way, it would be easier to launch the dinghy among the rocks and leave Dark Island and return to our sailboat.

I discovered some matches in my pocket, so we gathered some driftwood and made a fire for ourselves on the sand. Neither of us talked; there seemed to be nothing left to say or do.

After a while, the silence and the waiting got to me. I wandered off on a little walk by myself, leaving Gregg sitting hunched over on the sea chest, his head down, his hands in his pockets, humming a song to himself.

When I came back, Gregg greeted me with a casual wave of the hand.

"Guess what?" he said.

"What?"

"I opened the sea chest."

"You did not," I said. "That's impossible."

"No it's not, Christopher. I just pushed in part of the eagle and the lock opened right up."

"Hah."

Gregg shrugged. "I don't care if you don't believe me." He kicked the sand. "Nothing much was in there anyway."

I hesitated. If I asked Gregg what he found inside, it would sound as if I had changed my mind and now believed him.

"Ok," I said. "I'll play along with you. What was in the chest?"

Gregg shrugged his shoulders. "Just things," he finally said, in a puzzled tone. "Ordinary things."

"What do you mean?"

Gregg didn't answer.

I went over to the chest, pushed on the eagle and tried the lock. Nothing happened. I kicked at the wood. Nothing happened. When I turned around, Gregg was kneeling over a flat rock. He was holding something in the flat of his hand. I looked over his shoulder and saw from his empty palm that Gregg was holding a "pretend thing" which he saw only in his mind, but which was real to him.

"...And then I opened the sea chest," Gregg was saying, more to himself, I think, than to me. "... And all that was inside was a small wooden box, like Daddy has on his dresser."

Gregg lifted up the top of the pretend-box in his hand. "I opened the box, and took out the things inside it one by one, and put each one on this rock here, in a circle. First, there was a lady's thimble, like Grandmother had." He put the pretend-thimble on the rock. "Then a soldier's medal, with blue faded silk, like up at West Point." He placed the medal next to the thimble on the rock. "Then, a little copper oil can, as tall as my little finger... then an 1804 American half-cent... then, I think, a bracelet which some lady must have worn... and what was the last thing I put on the rock?"

He stared at the pretend-thing in his hand and then at the circle of pretend-things on the rock. "Oh, I know what it is; only I don't know its name." Gregg put that pretend-thing, too, down on the rock. Bracelet; old half-cent; tiny oil can; medal; thimble... and the other object without a name. For a long moment, the two of us crouched over the rock and looked down on that little circlet of things from another man's life, touched by Orlando's spirit and by the mystery of life and death. ◇

CHARLIE

(a true story)

BARBARA BRENT BROWER

"As a dyslexic," Barbara Brent Brower says, "I act as a role model for young people afflicted by this annoying mis-wiring."

She hasn't let dyslexia prevent her from achieving considerable success as a writer. Her work has been published in many journals and anthologies, including Snowy Egret, The Muse Strikes Back, The Jewish Spectator, *and* Grrrrr—A Collection of Poems About Bears. *She has three children, all of them successful in their chosen fields. "Charlie" was originally published in* Tirra Lirra, *in Australia.*

I was inside the house only once. Thanksgiving, 1963. It may still stand on that hill in Maryland, overlooking post-card perfect pastures full of cows lazily chewing their cud and horses racing along white rail fences.

The events of my day and night spent in that pre-Civil War

pile of hand-made brick covered with oyster shell stucco, supported by cypress trunks too thick to encircle with your arms; the feeling of palpable sadness in those echoing, empty rooms; the tower with its secret stairs, and in particular, the attic with its huge iron ring bolted to the floor; the aura of that house and Charlie, haunt me to this day.

The house belonged to friends who had purchased the property as a long-term investment. After receiving estimates of over one million dollars to restore the old house and add electricity, running water and plumbing, they decided to let it die a natural death and rent the land to neighboring farmers. On weekends and other special occasions they would "camp out" there and that is how I came to spend that most unusual Thanksgiving.

The day began with a beautiful drive from Washington, D.C., through Maryland's famous hunt country. The weather report had mentioned the possibility of a storm later in the day, but we drove through late fall sunrise that turned maples to flames and oaks to golden watchmen.

As we rounded the final bend in the country road, I caught my first glimpse of the brooding structure that crowned the highest hill in the landscape. The house looked exactly like one of Charles Addams's creations. The long, serpentine lane leading up to the house gave me the distinct feeling of traveling through a time warp into another century. I could almost hear the crunch of hoofs on the gravel and the jingle of harnesses as the car slowed to a stop and I stepped out to look directly at this structure that had absolutely nothing in common with the modern world.

We unpacked our gear and the groceries for our feast. Then we lugged the heavy battery-operated charcoal rotisserie to the East front lawn and started our small hen turkey turning on the spit. After everything was set up and we could smell the charcoal smoke beginning to perform its magic, my friends took me on an inspection tour of their much-loved pile of brick.

The steps to the verandah that circled the house were weather-worn. The second step was missing. The verandah itself was wide and inviting. I imagined it was a wonderful place to sit and rock and watch the world go past when the house was new and untouched by tragedy.

Heavy carved oak double doors groaned as they opened onto a huge central hall. Opposite the front door were French doors leading to the living room. On either side of the hall were spiral staircases leading to landings with balconies, where chamber orchestras once provided music for couples dancing below. Four additional steps gave way to the second floor hall and bedrooms and to another, shorter staircase, to the tower study. Back stairs led from the kitchen to the attic. Fifteen vacant rooms (including the servants' quarters, country basement, attic, and tower room) greeted us with old-house sighs, echoes and accumulated dust.

The only room that was habitable was the living room with its enormous fireplace. My friends had brought in some old furniture to make this single room a haven in the midst of the decay. We placed our sleeping bags on the floor in front of the fireplace before starting our tour.

"You know what I forgot to bring? A flashlight! Do you have one? With no electricity, we might need one later..."

My friends laughed. "We used to bring one, but now we love the dark of the place and the firelight. You'll get used to it."

We left the living room, crossed the central hall and climbed the West staircase to the tower study. The study was a fascinating room with a splendid three-sided view of the surrounding countryside. A moveable panel in one wall revealed a secret staircase leading to the roof. I wanted to try it, but my friends told me it wasn't safe, so, reluctantly, I followed them back down the stairs. But for a moment, when the panel slid open and I peered up into the narrow space, I thought I felt... something... a presence there.

"What a great place to play hide and seek!" I said, as the panel slid shut.

"We found some old marbles on the top step when we first went through the place. Someone quite small must have used the stairs as a secret play room," my friend's husband said as we left the tower.

We returned to the central hall and then climbed the East stairs to the bedrooms and then up the back stairs to the attic.

The attic had windows fitted into dormers on all four sides making it unusually light. It was empty except for a thick iron ring that was bolted to the center of the floor. My friends explained that, according to the former owners, the house had been built by a wealthy family in 1842. Sometime after the Civil War, the youngest son "turned odd in the head and began to have fits." He wasn't considered dangerous, but he had a habit of wandering away, so he was chained, for long periods of time, to the ring in the attic. Servants would bring him meals and attend to his needs, but he was otherwise left alone. His name was Charles Anthony, but everyone called him Charlie.

"Fiction! Pure fiction!" I exclaimed. "That story is straight out of *Jane Eyre*! People didn't actually do things like that to others... did they?" I paused because I suddenly had the feeling we were not alone. I shook the feeling off by looking around and assuring myself we were alone in the attic. "Odd, the tricks the mind can play," I thought.

"No. You are making that up just to put some mystery into this grand old place. It is a pity that you can't save it. There is something really appealing about this house. I pick up a residue of sadness, but this is a wonderful house. I envy you being able to come here to visit so often."

As I spoke I felt a slight modulation of temperature near the ring, like a breeze from an open window. But the windows were all shut. The feeling was not unpleasant, simply a change in the atmosphere.

We left the attic by way of the back stairs. My friends were silent for the first time that day and I wondered if they too had felt the change in the attic. We followed the stairs past pure desolation and decay. The roof over the rear of the building, a wing that did not include the attic, had fallen into the bedrooms on the East side leaving the flooring exposed to the elements. Over the years, the dampness had caused the ceiling in the kitchen to fall, except for one superb Della-Robia wreath of corn and wheat that somehow held to the wood lathing. I begged my friends to find a way to save that piece of the house if they could not save anything else. Over and over I found myself exclaiming about the beauty of the place, what it must have been like, how terrible it was to let it die. We wandered through the back rooms of the main floor until we came again to the central hall and then went out those massive double doors.

I was relieved to be back in fresh air and light and away from the dust, decay and inexplicable feeling of being watched.

Settled on the lawn on the East side of the house we had a spirited time telling tales of other old places we had visited, those with long, romantic histories. The homes in and around Waterford, Virginia, were of special interest as they were reputed to be haunted.

This visit, so far, had been a delightful experience shared with dear friends. The food, when it finally got done, was perfect. We ate, drank, and told stories until the weather took a sudden ugly turn and we were forced to sprint to the shelter of the house, carrying our feast with us. As I ran, I glanced up at the attic window. Storm cloud shadows made it seem, for the blink of an eye, that a face looked down on us from behind the rain-streaked glass.

Soaked to the skin, we quickly changed into dry clothes and

settled near the roaring fire to continue our meal and our tales until it grew very late and we retired for the night, our only light coming from the fireplace. Outside, the storm raged and shook the old house like a terrier shakes a rabbit.

Sometime before dawn, I had to go to the bathroom. To do that I had to leave what comfort there was by the embers of the hearth, cross the cavernous central hall in the pitch-black, find my way to the front door, follow the verandah around to the back and from there race to the outhouse.

As I closed the living room doors and began to cross the hall (muttering to myself about forgetting my flashlight), a crack of lightening illuminated the stairs and balconies. On the East balcony, peering down into the darkness was the shape of a man leaning over the balcony. I froze. A vagrant who was hiding in the house? We had seen no footprints but our own in the dust. No telltale signs of illicit habitation. I concluded that we were, indeed, alone in this place. Once the shock of the sight on the balcony subsided a bit, I realized that I did not feel threatened in any way, simply observed. Inspected. I hesitated. I thought about screaming. I thought about running back into the living room and waking my friends. Then I thought: "What a silly goose you are, spooking at shadows!" I forced myself across the rest of the expanse to the heavy front doors, not daring to look up again at the East balcony.

I had time to consider what I thought I had just seen as I sprinted through thunder, lightening and downpour to the outhouse and back.

I am a level-headed person, not given to hallucinations, and while up to that moment, had never met a ghost—wasn't sure I believed in them—I was willing to admit that there *are* phenomena that defy logic. It might have been the power of suggestion. We had been talking about the collective memory of old houses that certain sensitive people sometimes notice and telling some famous ghost stories during our evening by the fire.

It might have been the odd effect of the lightning casting shadows on the peeling plaster of the walls through the window of the East balcony. It might have been many things, but by the time I again stood before those massive doors, I was convinced (and still am convinced) that I saw a man in a long-sleeved white open-necked shirt and dark breeches looking over the balcony rail at me as I crossed the central hall.

I decided to confront whatever it was by speaking to it when I got back inside, whether it was still there or not.

My knees were quicksand, my teeth chattered like ice against glass and water dripped from my hair and clothes as I inched my way to the center of that coal mine of a center hall. I tried to adjust my voice to a level, not of terror, but of congeniality, as I faced the East balcony.

My first attempt got lost before it left my mouth. I cleared my throat and began again.

"I have heard many stories of you, Charles Anthony, or may I call you Charlie? I have come in peace and the spirit of friendship to visit your lovely home. I will be gone later this morning. Thank you for your hospitality." I found it difficult to breathe.

Another flash of lightning lit the space and I looked up. He was there—small and shy seeming: a boy-of-a man. He raised his right arm and waved, once, and was gone in the returning blackness. I stood rooted to the floor, trembling from the cold and another feeling, a feeling of accomplishment and discovery. Finally shaking free from the spell cast by this experience, I ran the rest of the way to the living room and woke my friends. They were delighted rather than frightened.

"He must like you. Probably because you have expressed such love for this house. Very few of our guests have actually *seen* Charlie, but everyone who spends more than a few hours here feels his presence. We have only seen him a few times ourselves. He is very shy, and, we think, quite lonely. We don't believe he ever had a real friend in his short, sad life."

I sputtered, "But why didn't you tell me you had a resident ghost? A moment ago I nearly had a stroke, I thought there was a tramp in this house just waiting to... well, then I realized that we had been all through this house and there really isn't anyone here but the three of us . . is there? I really saw Charlie? You know, after that first shock, I wasn't as scared as I was curious. But you should have warned me."

My friends looked amused. "Would you have believed us if we had told you? We've learned *not* to say anything. That way we can't be accused of planting thoughts in your head if you *do* see or feel something, or making up a story just for effect, if Charlie chooses not to appear."

I smiled. "You are very wise, come to think of it, and *very* fortunate. To own a house with such a sweet spirit attached to it is very rare!"

The house may still be there, although I know by now it would be more a ruin than a house. But I believe that Charlie will always be there, clinging to the last bit of brick, looking for a friend. ◊

MORE THAN MUSIC

LENORA K. ROGERS

Lenora K. Rogers has been published in many small press magazines, both literary and genre. Her latest work appears in The Midnight Gallery, The Edge, *and* Alien Worlds. *Work is forthcoming in* Bare Bones, Outer Darkness, *and* Anotherealm. *She lives in Summerville, South Carolina, and is currently working on a novel.*

The day was chilly, wet. Emmeline waited tensely at an upstairs window for news of Hugh. From the window, she had an unobstructed view of the gates at the end of the long drive. Anyone with a message for her would have to enter here.

It would likely be Hugh's younger brother Sam who came to tell her, if anyone came. And if no one came, then it would surely signify that Hugh had improved, that the fever had broken.

Hugh had taken ill on Friday, after a hunting trip. The weather had been miserable. He'd had a mild cold for several days but thought he was getting better. She had reminded him that her

Uncle Charles had died after a similar outing, taken too soon following a bout of influenza. Hugh had merely laughed and told her not to worry, that he was young and strong.

She thought of her birthday, just a week away. She would be nineteen. Her mother had married at nineteen. Emmeline, however, did not think she herself would marry so soon. Still, there was her hope chest, filled with table linens and bureau runners.

Two weeks ago she and Hugh had gone to the fair and Hugh had kissed her with great passion while they were on the Ferris wheel, high above everything. It had given her a grand revelation, the sudden knowledge that love eclipsed everything in one's life.

Her father came to the door of the room. "Sam Creighton is here to see you."

Her heart leaped to her chest. She jerked her head toward the window. How could she have missed his arrival? Had she been daydreaming? But there below stood the wagon with the two chestnut horses hitched to it, swishing their restless tails.

Emmeline hurried down the stairs.

Sam was sixteen, a timid, gangly boy. He stood waiting for her, gripping his hat in his hands.

"The doctor said to fetch you," he said to Emmeline as she entered the room.

Briefly, she put her hand to her mouth. "Oh... I see. Is he very bad?"

The boy's lips tightened. "I'd say so."

Emmeline looked away. "I'll just get a wrap." she said then. "I'll only be a minute."

They rode mostly in silence, with Sam urging the horses steadily along. Emmeline felt strangely empty inside. Not a tear welled in her eyes when she thought of Hugh. Losing him was the very thing she had feared, but now that the moment was upon her she was blank and unaffected by it. It was as if Hugh had already left her, already passed into the realm beyond. She imagined his funeral, the dark-suited mourners, the tombstone on his grave. And she imagined herself being courted again by her old flame Owen West.

"Whoa!" Sam ordered the horses. They had reached the Creighton house.

A feeling of dread settled upon Emmeline. She came near to asking Sam to take her back home. But he wouldn't have understood.

They went inside. A strong medicinal odor pervaded everything. Emmeline thought she would retch. She pressed her handkerchief to her nose.

"They've got him in the front room," Sam explained. "It's warmer in there."

Emmeline winced at the thought of the parlor being turned into a sickroom. She and Hugh had spent many happy hours here. They had played cards and put together jigsaw puzzles. She had picked out tunes on the piano for him and they had sometimes sung songs together, Hugh's favorite being "In the Gloaming."

A bed had been brought into the room and Hugh, sunk deep into the covers of it, was barely visible. She could see only his face, pale and still, like a mask.

Emmeline stopped across the room, not wanting to venture closer. The doctor, at the bedside, turned and calmly reassured her. "It's all right. You may come and speak to him. Perhaps he'll respond to your voice."

Emmeline crept up to the bed. "Hugh?" she murmured. "Hugh?"

His eyes did not open. He did not stir. There was no indication he had even heard her.

Sam stepped up beside her and leaned over the blankets and shook his brother's shoulder. "Hugh! Emmeline's here! Wake up!"

Slowly, Hugh's eyes opened. He gazed up at Emmeline. His breathing, though labored, seemed to quicken at the sight of her.

"Hello, Hugh," she said to him, her voice quavering badly.

"Em," he replied weakly. "Em—come closer."

Someone brought a chair for her.

"Give me your hand, Em," he said to her, struggling to bring his own from under the covers.

She placed her hand on top of his. It was cold, so cold it made her tremble in terror. It was as if death already had a grip upon him, had already taken over his extremities.

"Emmeline, I'm going to die..."

"Oh, no, Hugh!" she protested. "Never!"

He studied her with his fevered eyes. "Emmeline, you can't marry anyone else— promise me you won't."

"Oh...Hugh..." A sob tangled itself in her words. Her free hand reached for her throat.

"I will haunt you—haunt you forever—if you court another man after I'm gone."

Tears ran down her cheeks. She wanted to turn away but knew she couldn't.

"Promise me!" he demanded hoarsely. And his cold, dry hand suddenly asserted itself, springing to life and reaching out to clutch the folds of her dress.

Emmeline cried out, leaning back so quickly that the chair nearly toppled over behind her.

The doctor interceded. "It's too much for her," he said. "Take her outside, Sam."

She leaned heavily upon Sam's arm as they left the room. She could hear Hugh struggling to speak, to keep her there with his words. "You're only mine, Emmeline—remember that.

You're not to marry..."

Outside the room, Sam attempted to calm her. "Don't take it to heart, what he says—it's just the fever making him talk like that."

She stood facing the wall, the little roses in the wallpaper all running together through her tears. She didn't want Sam to watch her cry.

He waited patiently through her silence and grief.

Then finally, clearing his throat, he said to her, "Anyway, you don't believe in ghosts, do you Emmeline?"

It had been four months since Hugh's death. Emmeline had gotten over her loss and had begun to go out among friends and acquaintances again. She had not forgotten what Hugh had told her on his deathbed, but she no longer entertained thoughts of marriage, in any case. She would be a maiden lady, like Aunt Ida. She would live with her parents until they passed on, and then she would live by herself. At Christmas, she would visit her two brothers' families and dote on her nieces and nephews. Her life would be full enough without marriage.

Then one night, as she was clearing the dishes from the table, there was a knock at the front door. Moments later, her mother entered the kitchen, flustered but smiling. "It's Owen West, dear— he's come to call on you. Do come out and sit with him awhile. I'll finish up here."

Emmeline, though pleased to see her old beau, felt shy and uncertain around him. She could only answer his questions in the briefest of terms: Was she feeling better these days? —Yes. Had she been skating on the pond lately? —No. Did she not find Reverend Cobb's sermon last Sunday rather tiresome? —Well, somewhat.

It wasn't until he began to tell her of the antics of his new bulldog pup that Emmeline warmed to his presence. She smiled and even laughed as he mimicked the sounds of the new puppy.

Before he left her that evening, he took both her hands and said, "It's wonderful to see you again, Emmeline. May I call on you this Saturday? Perhaps we could go out to the pond and skate."

"I would like that, yes," Emmeline replied.

He did not kiss her but briefly stopped at the door and, turning again to her, uttered her name in the old, familiar way he had done when they first courted.

For some moments after he had gone, Emmeline stood by the door, entranced, unable to think of anything but Owen's playful grey eyes and the tender warmth of his hands.

Then her mother called out suddenly, as though something had happened.

Jarred from her reverie, Emmeline hurried to the kitchen. "What is it, Mother?"

Mrs. Danforth stood staring at the far window, a puzzled look on her face. "I don't know, dear. I thought I saw a face just now, looking in at me from the outside—perhaps one of those hobos from town. It was quite startling."

Emmeline went to the window and peered at the panes of glass. Nothing but the darkness of night pressed against them. "I don't see anything, Mother," she said.

Her mother, undaunted, chuckled. "Well, then, it's only my imagination, I suppose."

But Emmeline was quiet, thinking of something else as she left the kitchen.

On her way down the hall, she stopped abruptly at the parlor door, entered the room and sat down at the piano. She played "In the Gloaming" through several times, humming the melody softly, hearing the words in her mind: *When the winds are sobbing faintly with a gentle, unknown woe, Will you think of me and love me, As you did once long ago?"*

It was her hope that the song would placate Hugh, if indeed he intended to come back and haunt her. Still, there was no proof that the face in the window had been his, or even that there had been a face in the window. But it wouldn't hurt to take some precaution.

O wen West came regularly now to sit with Emmeline in the little parlor. And just as regularly, after his departure, Emmeline would slip back into the parlor and play "In the Gloaming" on the piano.

Though the piano was old and produced a tinny sound when she played it, Emmeline breathed a sigh of relief each time the ritual was completed. And it was working, she thought. No specter, after all, had appeared to cause her harm; Hugh rested quietly in his grave. All was well.

One night, after she had once again played Hugh's favorite song on the parlor piano, Emmeline's father, looking up from his book, remarked, "You could play a livelier tune than that one, Em."

"Yes, I suppose," Emmeline replied vaguely. She had never told her parents of Hugh's deathbed threat. Little did they suspect the real reason she so often played this sentimental song. But it was more than music to her now —it was her shield against the unknown, her sole source of protection against the phantom that would steal her life away.

"There's not some sadness weighing heavily upon you, then?" her father inquired.

"No—of course not," Emmeline assured him.

"Good," her father grunted, going back to his book.

She had gone to stay a few days with Aunt Ida, who had fallen and sprained her ankle.

Sitting in a chair by the fireplace, her foot propped on a stool, Aunt Ida entertained Emmeline with rollicking tales of her girlhood days. Emmeline enjoyed the time spent with Aunt Ida, but she was eager to return home, eager to see Owen. As soon as her aunt could hobble around without danger of hurting herself again, she packed up her clothes and sent word to her father to come and get her.

To her surprise and delight, Owen was waiting for her on the front porch when she arrived home. "Your mother told me you were coming," he said, holding out a small box of candy to her. "Welcome back."

"Oh, how thoughtful of you," Emmeline said, accepting his gift.

They went inside, where her mother steered them all toward the dining room. "I've made a big dinner," she announced. "I hope everyone is hungry."

Emmeline was tired after the long ride home and so Owen did not stay long after they'd eaten. But he kissed her lovingly at the door before leaving and promised he would come again very soon.

It was the kiss and the touch of his hands upon her that necessitated "In the Gloaming" on the piano. These were the things, she felt, that would most offend Hugh, that could bring him back to haunt her. And what would happen when Owen proposed marriage to her? Would she have to play the song through twenty times to be completely safe? Fifty?

She stopped beside the parlor door and sighed with determination. Once again, she must ward off Hugh's ghost.

The door was already ajar. She pushed it further open and went inside.

The lamp had not been lit but the room was softly illuminated by the light from a full moon. She gazed at the windows momentarily, thinking of Owen, and then turned to the task of playing Hugh's music.

But where was the piano? The spot it had occupied was bare.

Emmeline's breath came in short gasps. She rushed to the vacant space and stood staring in disbelief at the emptiness.

Her mother came to the doorway, looking for her. "Are you in here, dear?"

Emmeline could not reply.

Her mother spotted her and came into the room. When she saw Emmeline standing in the empty space, she said, "Oh, I meant to tell you earlier— we sold the piano while you were gone. A very good price we got for it too, considering its age. You don't mind, do you, dear? Such a shabby old thing." She paused and reflected. "He was quite a nice young man, though not from these parts. Reminded me a bit of your Hugh, God rest him. But I can't figure out for the life of me how he knew we had a piano."

Emmeline began to scream. ◊

THE CHILL OF AN EARLY FALL
TERRY CAMPBELL

Terry Campbell describes himself as "a 37-year old writer / artist living in Terrell, Texas, until my wife and I can escape to the country." He seeks inspiration in old cemeteries, stormy weather, and Jefferson, Texas, "the most haunted town in the state." His stories have appeared in Horrors! 365 Scary Stories, Cemetery Sonata, *and* Kiss and Kill: the Hot Blood Series. *He is also a staff artist for* Flesh and Blood *and* Outer Darkness.

The rickety old bait stand looms over the pier like a trusted sentinel, its clapboard siding greyed a shade darker by another season of summer rains and salt spray blown in from the Atlantic, its windows boarded up for another seven long months. Hanging from its rafters, creaking and swaying in the late afternoon breeze, a sign announces the sale of fishing licenses and bait by the quart. Beyond the tired old shack, the empty pier sits languidly in the threshold of the shallow surf, the shadows of the posts and ropes stretching almost endlessly across the wooden planks. The golden sunset spits a warm, lush glow across the beachfront scene but, despite the cozy colors that engulf the perpetual landmarks, the approaching chill in the gentle winds cannot be denied. From deep across the horizon, steel grey storm clouds stretch ever closer to the tiny island resort, signaling the end of another season and the onset of winter.

She stands at the bridge that had carried hundreds of tourists to the pier, her bare toes cool in the shifting sands. A smattering of many gulls blends with the steady drone of the wind and the lazy splash of the waves lapping against the pier supports, and if she closes her eyes, she can almost imagine summer still surrounds her.

She turns her head northward, brushing wisps of golden hair from her pale face, and peers up the coast line. The winter mists are already beginning to engulf the island; she can barely make out the outer edges of the coast of Massachusetts. All of the tourists are gone now. The lifeblood of the land has ebbed back to the mainland, leaving the desolate island to sleep its winter slumber.

During the summer, the island is a thriving tourist attraction. The warm waters, the sandy beaches, the rolling, floral hillsides attract the throngs in masses: families, fishermen, artists, writers. The little island teems with laughter, color, and merriment from April through September. Fishing boats are chartered for hours-long bouts with sailfish, tuna, and the occasional shark. Families picnic along the miles and miles of white sandy beach. Artists and their easels dot the island from the coastline to the forests and up into the hills. The activities extend from the early morning hours into the late night. The island is a pleasant place to be, filled with the sounds of people enjoying life.

A gust of wind blows ocean mist into her face, and she has to hold her dress down in the brisk breeze. She shudders. Every gust of wind seems to lower the temperature a few more degrees. The island is empty now, save for the remote few, the locals who somehow manage to blunder their way through the drab, grey months of winter. As the warmth of the summer sun departs, so does life seem to leave the island. Similarly, the icy winds of chill are the harbingers of death.

The island itself becomes lifeless and grey upon the arrival of winter. The aquamarine waves roll and churn to a monochromatic taupe. The once-bright skies are transformed to a monotonous ashen shade. The trees are all stripped bare. The lush green hills, now devoid of chlorophyll, turn a drab brown. Winter brings with it a sheer, plastic sheeting, grey in color, and drapes it over the land.

She steps over the chain railing along the sidewalk, and begins to make her way up the coastline. Hundreds of fallen leaves, colored a familiar earth tone, bounce and dance down the asphalt toward the ocean, sounding like the legs of thousands of tiny lobsters stampeding to the sea. The trees stretch their naked, scrawny arms toward the dismal sky. A single leaf, struggling valiantly to cling to its mother branch, loses its battle and tumbles to the clammy ground in pursuit of its siblings. She wants to cry, but cannot.

She continues down the sidewalk past the inn, the white-washed building that had held so many happy tourists during previous months. Now, the only sign of life inside the colonial structure is a lamp glowing in the window of the sitting room. She moves past the inn, through the heart of town, pausing solemnly to inspect each boarded window. Through the knotholes she peers, inspecting the insides of the deserted shops, the winter dusts already settling on the once-cheery interiors.

Past the outskirts of town, the lay of the land begins to take on a slight incline, but she does not notice. She strays from the sidewalk, cutting through the brown weeds, the blades of faded grass feeling cold and lifeless to her bare feet. She labors slightly as she descends the grassy hill, trudging past the sight where so many painters had set up their easels to create their oil and acrylic renditions of birch trees, Devil's paintbrushes, and colorful wildflowers. Now, the hill is as barren and lifeless as the paintings that were created. She wants to cry, but cannot.

At last, the brown covering of grass gives way to the pale sands of the beach, and she continues on in her circle of the island. Hundreds of gulls strut and hop along the shoreline, conducting their final cleaning of summer scraps left behind by the tourists. She wants to smile at their hapless guffawing, but she can't find it in her being to show happiness in the face of the lifeless winter.

Out on the ocean, a lone scalloper makes its way back toward the pier, the sole occupant of a vast stretch of water that so recently had been filled with countless multi-colored sails. Now, only the scalloper remains, and soon, it too, is gone. The only evidence that distinguishes the ocean's surface from an expanse of grey carpet is the constant parade of rolling whitecaps. She wants to cry, but cannot.

She lowers her head, momentarily enthralled by the way the fine granules tumble down the slopes of her feet when her weight presses into the sand. She lets the whine of the winds, the roar of the ocean, and the shrill cries of the seabirds meld together until they are but one dull cacophony of winter noises.

She stops at the ramshackle bait stand. Her trip has come full cycle. It is time to go home, just as the tourists, and indeed, the thrill of life have gone. She shuffles past the bait stand toward the water's edge.

Yes, for the season, life has left the tiny island. As robustly as life embraced the island in summer, so terribly does the essence of death grip it in winter. No outsider could know the island as it is in winter. No one knows how bitter is the night, how fiercely blows the wind, how dreary are the skies, how dark grows the mind.

The island is not without tourists in the winter, but they are certainly visitors of a different sort. Ask any family of mother, father, and 2.3 kids who visited the island during the previous winter season. Question any chartered fishing boat hauling its jubilant catch of bluefin, and no one aboard could tell of the locals who must scrape out their living, of the weathered fishermen who must brave the fierce winter sea for a meager bounty of lobster during the cold winter months, after the happy tourists have returned to their gay mainland lives. Ask any budding Rembrandt splashing bright swatches of pastels across a pre-stretched canvas, and he would know nothing of his winter counterpart who spends long bone-chilling months uninspired in front of a blank canvas gripping a single tube each of black and white paint, endlessly mixing various shades of grey on his palette, forever searching for, but never finding, color. None of them would know what happens on this tiny island when the season of death engulfs it.

Just as the sun and its warmth bring the carefree masses of people to life, so the dark icy grip of winter brings the dead to the island. The dead come to revel in the cold, bone-chilling winds, to circle the empty shell of an island, and to ponder their lonely existence, the only existence they know, in the netherworld.

She turns to glance once more at the weathered bait stand, the sound of the rusted bait sign still audible from this distance. She strains her ears and, for a moment, she can almost hear them: the cries of the children, the laughter of the adults, the bustle of life. *Summer sounds.* But it's only the wind. Only the wind.

She turns back to the grey ocean, its murky depths beckoning her back to her home. The tide assails the beach with more ferocity than even moments earlier, claiming any lingering evidence of summer and carrying it back to its frigid lair. Death grips the island in the cold of winter. Death owns all in the grey void.

She wants to cry, but cannot.

Only the living can cry. ◊

HERRICK'S INN

SCOTT THOMAS

Scott Thomas's fiction has appeared in numerous publications, such as DAW's The Year's Best Horror Stories #22, The Dead Inn, Leviathan 3, Haunts, The Silver Web, Deathrealm, Lore, The Urbanite, Flesh and Blood, redsine, Penny Dreadful, *and* Black Rose. *Delirium Books published his collection of old fashioned ghosts and horrors from which two stories were reprinted in St. Martin's* The Year's Best Fantasy and Horror #15. *His artwork is available on T-shirts and note cards from Gravestone Artwear, in Maine (and on the web).*

He lives with his wife, Nancy, in Massachusetts.

Sudbury, Massachusetts — 1757

Spring had come to the woods behind the inn—the evidence was both subtle and grand. Fiddleheads poked up from the damp, dark earth at the edge of a pond like the unfurling tails of tiny submerged dragons. Flowering trees stood in the midst of their bare grey counterparts, radiant bonnets of pink in the lowering afternoon light. Breezes rustled the dry brown carpet of leaves that winter had left behind, as dusk brought a coolness that might have passed for September. But this was the first of May, and lovers met in the quiet spring wood.

Rebecca Herrick was the innkeeper's only surviving daughter. The other three had perished ten years previous when Rebecca was a young girl. Consumption had come reaping. Now, at eighteen, she was her father's prize, and was it any wonder? She was an angelic creature, her hair an amber spill framing the rounded pallor of her face. Her features were fine and her figure appealingly plump. Her father did his best to keep her in the kitchen, safely away from the eyes of the lonely travelers that frequented the inn.

The father had failed in keeping John Easty from noticing the girl. The young doctor's apprentice, who had been visiting an ill brother in Grafton, was on his way back to Boston when he stopped at Herrick's Inn. It was December dusk and a sluggish snow had fallen on the round New England hills, had whispered into the grey woods. The old inn had been a welcome sight, its windows warm and gold. The innkeeper's daughter had been a welcome sight as well.

Warming by the fire, John had watched as the girl went about her serving duties in the tavern room. She was graceful and sweet and her laughter had a lilting quality as it rose up into the dark beams above. Some months later a drunken miller would put inappropriate hands on the lass. She was consigned to the kitchen following the episode, the miller chased off with a musket.

Subsequent visits to the Herrick Inn followed. John courted Rebecca, unbeknownst to her father. At first they met in the woods behind the inn, but later John climbed a tree by the house and stole into her bedchamber. They spent several nights together.

Now, under the cool, darkening May sky, the lovers embraced

within their shelter of trees, a tethered horse nearby. John could smell the kitchen smoke in Rebecca's hair as he pressed her to his chest. Her belly was against his, soft and warm—it was not the hard pouting thing it had been during his last visit.

Rebecca's parents had never even noticed that she had been carrying a child. Her plumpness, apron, and the full skirts common to the day, had kept the fact secret.

"It was dead at birth," Rebecca said in a whisper.

"Oh, dear," John groaned, holding her tighter.

"Not to worry, I buried him in a lovely spot and said prayers."

"A boy?"

Rebecca nodded against him. She felt him shiver. She said, "Please do not fret. It's for the best, in actual fact. Father would have done away with me, if ever he knew."

John agreed quietly.

Rebecca pulled back and looked up. She gave him a fetching smile and touched his cheek. "We are together, nothing matters so much as that."

John took her hand and kissed it. "Yes. That *is* what matters."

They moved slowly toward the inn and its outbuildings, the icehouse dark and windowless in the gloom. Geese flew honking over a willow and a breeze rattled the leafy carpet.

"You must wait until you see my parents' window go dark," Rebecca reminded the man. "My window shall be unlocked."

"Unlocked, yes, of course—I shouldn't want to break it," he joked.

Rebecca squeezed his hand. "I've missed you so," she said, and then she headed off across the small grassy field that separated the woods from the back of the inn.

When the last of the laughter had died away in the tavern and the last guest had staggered up to his room, Rebecca hurried in to sweep the floor and wipe the ale-scented tables. Her hair, loosened from under her bonnet by the steam in the kitchen, hung in her face.

She straightened the chairs and made certain that the logs were safely positioned in the hearth before taking up a candle and climbing the stairs to her own quarters. The inn was quiet at this late hour, but for some muffled snoring, heard as she passed the guest rooms.

In her chamber, she set the candle down by the bed and quickly, though cautiously, unlocked and partly opened her window. She had taken to keeping it shut in all weather since strange noises had started to come from the woods, some weeks back.

Rebecca removed her bonnet, combed out her long hair and pinched her cheeks to give them color. She could hear sounds coming from outside, someone moving slowly up the great old maple that grew close to the house. Smiling, she removed her garments and tossed them aside, unceremoniously. The air gave her a chill. She slid into the bed, pulling the covers to her throat, resting her head back on the pillow that she had used to smother the baby.

While the candle was largely burnt down, the wick could have used a trimming, and the flame burned too high. The glare on the glass prevented her from making out the vague figure that was now pushing open the window.

John stood in the dark wood, stomping in place to keep warm, as one by one the windows in the distant inn went dark. The chill made him restless, made him imagine the heat of Rebecca's body.

The leaves rattled somewhere, and once he turned and thought that he saw a small hunched animal duck behind a tree— a skunk or a raccoon, likely. Animals sounded in the dim expanse of tangled trees. Living in the city, he had grown unaccustomed to the sounds of wildlife, had forgotten how some birds could sound like a baby crying.

Another window went dark—the window that belonged to the innkeeper and his wife. Grinning, John stepped out from the edge of the wood, into the small field.

Light glowed in Rebecca's room. He had reached the inn, old and somber-looking, rambling—the ancient structure added to over the years, grown out from its original humble size. There were several scraggly lilac bushes along the base of the structure, their purple flowers just days from blooming. The stately maple loomed, reached up past Rebecca's open window, towered over the roof.

John grunted as he hefted himself into the lower branches. There were a good many sturdy limbs to climb on—no worse than a ladder. The window was close, he could see the candlelight wavering on the ceiling of the room. He heard something as well, but he could not readily identify the sound. Was it slurping?

Successful at last, John gripped the edge of the open window and pulled himself up. He looked in at the bed, at Rebecca dead and naked upon it, with a small grey form crouched on her belly. Its hairless head was round, and it stopped nursing to turn and glare at him. It hissed.

Somehow John managed not to scream. He scrambled awkwardly down the tree and fell several feet from the bottom. He ran to where his horse was tethered, just inside the dark wood, and spurred it swiftly to the road.

His heartbeat matched the pounding of the hooves, as the mare galloped along the road. Even when John closed his eyes he could see the baby's face, like a small rotting pumpkin, the disintegrating flesh lit softly, internally, as if by a chunk of the moon. Mostly he saw the eyes—darker than a skull's, darker than the night that his horse carried him into. ◊

THE FAMILY JEWEL
DIANALEE VELIE

Dianalee Velie's poetry and short stories have been published in hundreds of literary journals (such as Kalliope, The Potomac Review, *and* The South Dakota Review*); her poetry, plays and prose have won numerous awards. She is a graduate of Sarah Lawrence College and has a Master of Arts in Writing from Manhattanville College. She has taught creative writing courses in a number of colleges and universities—like her awards, too numerous to list in a one-volume anthology! Currently she teaches poetry, memoir or short story in the ILEAD program at Dartmouth, poetry at Adventures in Learning at Colby Sawyer College, and Contemporary American Poetry at the College for Life Long Learning.*

Filly watched the blizzard pile huge drifts of snow on the back deck. The view through the sliding doors was being quickly obliterated by the fierce diamond-edged white flakes hurling themselves against the glass with unabated fury. The white-out was unrelenting. Cold bitter winds cried through every crevice in the house, determined to help the storm pour out its rage.

She sat snuggled under her light blue afghan, content to keep the fire going nice and steady. Everyone was safe and sound. The boys were out of state with their father visiting Nana. They would not be happy to hear they had missed the snowstorm of the century. Her daughter, Lily, had come home early from the barn, having safely tucked Necromancer, her prized black stallion, under some extra blankets. He would spend the night safe and warm in his stall and in the morning would be eager to romp in the fresh white stuff covering the earth. As Filly played with the tiny tear-shaped iridescent crystal hanging around her neck on a thin gold chain, she felt serenely nostalgic. The evening reminded her so much of her own childhood in the country.

"Come here, pumpkin," she called out to Lily. "Let me help you get those riding boots off. I'm so glad you're home."

Filly got up and tugged on Lily's long black boots till they slid off her slender calves. Lily was watching the top of her mother's head as Filly bent over her daughter's boots. Filly fell back in playful exhaustion.

"Mom, you've gotten more white hair. Here let me pull this one out. It's sticking straight up, and besides, Clarissa's mother lets her pull out all her grey hairs."

"Then I'm surprised she's not bald already." Lily laughed and pushed her mother down onto the soft couch, plopping down next to her. Lily snuggled into her mother's arms, too much on her way to becoming a woman to fit into her lap, but still needing the warmth and softness of her touch.

Filly lovingly caressed and stroked her daughter's long brown curls. Her own hair was turning white just as Lily's would one day; the years really seemed to fly. This seemed like a good time to tell her the story of her great-, great-grandmother, Anna Patchenka.

"Do you know how those white hairs are placed Lily, and why and by whom?" Lily turned her head to face her mom, eager to hear another one of her mother's stories.

"They are settled there, one by one, by a very special spirit, and she is very close to you. She was my great-grandmother, Anna Patchenka, and she had the most beautiful green eyes, just like yours." Filly paused now, trying to pick her words very carefully. She did not want to tell Lily too much too soon. She remembered distinctly the awe she felt when she first saw the spirit of Anna Patchenka take shape. Even though the spirit world was rapidly gaining credibility and Lily had studied about it at school, this was a particularly strong spirit, and it guided every woman in their family. Spirituality was still not an easy thing to discuss between parent and child, but with the warmth and security of the fire shielding them from the storm, the moment seemed right. Besides, it was really past the time she should have spoken to Lily; and tonight was perfect.

"You see, my little one, life is really a balance, a fine white thread, a stability, that we must walk with open eyes, an open heart and always an open mind." She paused now to take a deep breath, much as her own mother had paused years ago when telling her the truth. She continued now with Lily's complete attention.

"We must always try to master the art of balancing all three, but it is only by imbalance that we acquire wisdom and the ability to cope with the unforeseen." Filly looked down at her daughter. She could tell by the quizzical expression on her face, that she still did not see the connection between this story and her mom's white hair. She took another deep breath and continued.

"Whenever life becomes too easy, or we become too complacent, the spirit of Anna Patchenka swoops down and pulls out the fine white thread of balance and places it gently into our crown of brown curls as we peacefully sleep. We wake up wiser and more serene, able to walk another fine white line that has already been laid down for us." Lily looked up at her mom; the look of mystery that had shrouded her face moments before had lifted. Filly was going to continue, but Lily's face was aglow with understanding.

"I think I've already seen the spirit, Mom. She comes to me sometimes when I'm riding Necromancer or have just finished a great paper for school. She always tells me I can do anything I set my mind on, no matter what my age. Oh Mom, she's a beautiful spirit. Her long white hair billows on the wind and she rides a fierce white stallion, always bareback. And oh, her face! It is so gentle and radiant and gorgeous, with deep blue eyes like pools of wisdom."

So her daughter had already seen the spirit of Anna Patchenka. Filly decided to finish her daughter's description. "And her body is as young and slender as yours and white as alabaster, and always proudly unclothed."

"Oh Mother, that's right! I have seen her. I have!" Lily was now up and waving her arms and dancing in jubilation. Filly beamed with pride. She was glad she had chosen this moment to tell her daughter, even if she had already seen the spirit. Anna Patchenka was obviously up to her old tricks, already laying out the fine white lines Lily would have to walk.

"Now come here a moment, little one. She is a strong and willful spirit and not easy to pacify. She will continue to test you by always removing the fine white thread just when you've thought you'd achieved perfect balance." Filly wrapped her arms around her daughter and they both snuggled under the well-worn blue afghan.

It really was time to throw another log on the fire. The room had begun to get chilly. The storm outside had subsided. The heavy black evening sky, sliding down to soothe the gentle white blanket on the earth, had turned into a warm grey with the light of the moon and the reflection of the snow. Occasional flurries floated daintily down from the heavens. The evening bore no resemblance to the earlier fury. The world was at peace.

Filly decided she had told her daughter enough about the spirit for now. As she gazed at the passionately blazing fire, she realized that one day soon she would have to tell her daughter the rest of the story. Lily would have to warn the men she loved, warn them to be true and faithful, for that lithe spirit, full of wonder and encouragement, was also an avenger. In their dreams, men chased her young form as she fled through the clouds on her white stallion. Most of them never really wanted to catch her; she was only a dream, but if they turn their fantasies into reality and cheat on the woman they love, the spirit of Anna Patchenka turns to face them. The face of a wizened old toothless hag, turns to stare at them from that wholesome young body and the steel blue eyes penetrate their very soul with guilt. With the sound of her one piercing scream, "Holeda," still ringing in their ears, they never wake up.

Hugging her daughter tighter and clutching her necklace, Filly decided this part of the story could wait. Lily would not see that side of the spirit until she had shed her one, first, perfect, crystal tear of sorrow, crying over a man. Filly would then pass the necklace to Lily so she too, like all the Patchenka women before her, would wear her tears like diamonds.

"Close your pretty green eyes, my little one, and just let me hold you. Right now you remind me so much of my great-grandmother." ◊

THE LODGE
SARAH C. HONENBERGER

Although Sarah C. Honenberger resides and practices law in Virginia, she spent summers at her grandmother's house in Marblehead and still visits Rockport once a year. This intimate knowledge of the Massachusetts coast has served her well, as evinced by the way she so superbly captures "a sense of place" in "The Lodge." Her writings, which have appeared in numerous literary journals (such as Antietam Review*) and elsewhere (*Oprah Winfrey Show*), have won a number of awards, and she herself has served as editor or judge for several literary venues.*

When a rich Boston banker paid the McLafferty brothers to build the Lodge, everyone in town talked incessantly of its grand purpose. Stories simmered and roiled, transforming the clear water of meager facts into a virtual whirlpool of embellished fairy tales. While the McLaffertys lived, the stories glinted with particles of truth, but their abbreviated descriptions tempted speculation. "Dolphin bath handles" or "Italian marble hearth" did not satisfy curious listeners.

Without admitting her true reason, Mrs. Porter set her famous rhubarb pies on the windowsill to entice Jimmy McLafferty. Between bites, he'd "yes, ma'am" her, eventually dropping a small detail that she worked into the next sewing circle, creating a pearl from his speck of sand. When she grew tired of that effort, she baked again. Mrs. Porter cooked up most of what folks thought they knew about the Lodge.

In 1931 the last McLafferty died, crazy as a loon from things he'd seen in the war. As the Lodge fell into disrepair, the tales grew wilder, and the yard went to seed. Some said the banker's bride raised four children there after he disappeared in the French Alps. Others spoke of an illegitimate daughter who ran away, causing her mother's untimely death from heartbreak. One story related the sons' greedy argument over the estate.

From summer to summer, the gardens spread over their rock borders, mixing nicotiana with the unkempt lawn. Neighbors wondered at the random appearance of clippings, patches of mended roof, and stretches of gleaming paint on rusted gutters. After the first cold snap of the season, an unseen yardman replaced the wooden screens with storm windows of the same vintage.

Wrapped securely in wide porches, the Lodge stood on Massachusetts granite. Thick doors braced an interior that no one except the McLaffertys had seen. Through fluttering curtains, passersby said they saw lamps glowing and shadowy shapes in the parlor. Every so often a hushed slip of conversation, a low hymn-like refrain, escaped to dance in summer breezes, floating above empty lawn chairs.

The front windows mirrored the ocean's sparkling blue. Salty breezes rocked the wicker chairs. In one swaying rocker, tourists claimed to see a grey-haired spinster doze, but glimpsing back, the chair was empty after all. Bewildered visitors returned to beachcombing, overlooking perfect shells, forgetful in their confusion. Furtive glances to the porch did not allay their suspicions about the disappearing lady. Eventually, though, the sunset distracted them. As with dreams, their recitations at dinner fell flat, indistinguishable from a general unsettled feeling.

In winter Boy Scouts, urged by their mothers, shoveled the walk. They huffed loudly at the lack of earthly reward. Distracted by their crisp smoking breath, they ended up in snowball wars, irregular encampments behind the rock walls. Joking good-naturedly, they barely noticed parted curtains and smoke wisps that trailed the roofline to drift into January's chill.

When a nor'easter bellowed out of the March sky, locals watched impatiently for someone to right the down-turned chairs and to straighten shutters yanked crooked by the fierce winds. Inevitably someone did but never while anyone was looking. The same someone dragged fallen branches into thick piles and left them to melt into the woods where the stone wall lost its definition to aspiring blackberries. Speculation said the phantom gardener arrived on the midnight train, departing before the town awakened. A policeman confirmed a midnight traveler, but the conductor simply shrugged and smiled.

One little girl named Mary Sullivan recounted a party of cookies and iced tea, complete with wrinkled faces and lace hankies. No one put much store in Mary's tale because her father drank—her unreliability, hereditary. Mary's description of pale peony bouquets became the town benchmark for eyebrow raising. Because Mary felt the shame of generations of immigrants, she vowed to expose the truth and vindicate her family in the eyes of her disdainful neighbors.

The Sullivans lived near the depot where Mr. Sullivan embarked each morning for the shoe factory, leaving behind his not insubstantial family. Four boys and two girls rose to his cheerful goodbye, scrambled to wash faces, and grabbed toast on their way to school. Mary was the youngest; her rosy cheeks and sparkling blue eyes a trick of the devil, many remarked, after they met her emaciated, sorrowful mother. Mary was her father's favorite. When the train puffed in at dusk, she met him, slipping her small hand into his callused one. Inebriated, he mixed up the crooked streets and would have walked into the ocean but for Mary. He brought in a steady sum, though, and turned it over to his wife who gave him a daily stipend which he spent before he returned each evening.

"Papa, you know how Katherine Ann pays for my piano lessons from her laundry money?" Mary asked.

"No, I didn't know, and from now on, I shall take care of it myself for my sweet girl." He jingled the pennies in his pocket as if they were gold.

"No, that's all right, Papa. I run the bundles back for her so I earn it myself."

"Ah, well, that's a smart girl too, you are."

"But my question, Papa? If someone offers you lemonade and cookies on the way home, and you're so thirsty you might die, and you've never been in their house, and it looks ever so interesting and different, is it all right to say yes?"

Bending down to scrutinize this miniature piece of perfection, Mr. Sullivan gazed into her eyes, gauging her intensity. Mary squeezed his hand to remind him that she waited. Parental concern should have prompted him to ask the owner's name, but he didn't, sensing that she would share it if she wanted him to know.

"Now, Mary dearest," he answered. "Only if your sister or mother know where you are. Never the house of a total stranger, and best not be too long or your mother'll worry." As he winked, her face relaxed into a smile.

"Thank you, Papa."

"Don't be thanking me, thank the lady who's baked the cookies. I'm hungry enough to eat them myself, Mary girl."

Friday Katherine Ann counted the laundry money and gave Mary her portion for the deliveries. Two coins in her pocket, Mary stuffed the piano book into her school satchel. She kissed her mother's cheek, warm and soft still from sleep. In the street the boys threw the ball, waiting for their little sister.

After school, instead of trailing behind the boys, Mary followed South Street to Miss Julia Worthington's parlor and her sternly polished grand piano. Eyeing the china plate covered with tiny sandwiches, the little girl took her place and began.

"Slower, Mary Sullivan, this is not a race. A piano, like a lady, ought to be serene and measured." Usually Mary played cautiously, eager for praise, but today, filled with anticipation, she rushed through as quickly as possible.

Miss Worthington wasn't through. "Once more, Miss Sullivan, then I must listen to that inept O'Houlihan child. Whatever is her name?"

Mary mouthed "Eloise" and continued to play her arpeggios.

"Very nicely done," the teacher said. "When you concentrate, you are quite a little musician. Off you go, Eloise awaits." Miss Julia curled her lips slightly upwards and her eyes danced so Mary knew she meant to smile.

Placing the money from her pocket in the wooden box, her big eyes watched the teacher close the lid. "Thank you, Miss Julia."

"Thank you, Miss Mary."

Satchel flying, Mary raced up South Street's long hill to the maple trees that shaded the Lodge's stone wall. Dark clouds piled up against the ancient limbs, rocking the highest branches and spilling an eerie grey light on the deserted yard. So intent was Mary on the slender form beckoning her from the granite stoop, she didn't notice the storm. Slipping into the dim hallway, she followed soft footsteps to the promised tea and cookies. A sudden gust of wind slammed the door shut behind her.

For two days and three nights, the ragged tempest rained down, littering the manicured lawns with broken branches, the beaches with mastless boats, and the roads with streaming torrents. Many later named the storm of 1915, a portent of war. In Sunday's early morning hours, the moon escaped its blackened prison, painting the debris with a silver ghostly glow. Mr. Sullivan woke in the corner booth of his favorite saloon. He'd drunk his entire paycheck. On the way home he prayed his wife had scrounged enough, in his absence, to feed his brood.

Katherine Ann, frantic about her little sister, dug out her father's hip boots and traipsed through the swirling water to the priest's house to telephone Miss Julia. The teacher, having housed Eloise O'Houlihan the entire week of the storm, had taken to her bed, but she answered Katherine Ann's question.

"Your Mary was in a great hurry on Friday, I will say. No, I didn't see which way she went." To the priest's discomfort, Katherine Ann burst into tears.

Police combed the streets and beaches, but offered little hope. A storm of this proportion carries off heavier things than a little girl. While the Sullivans grieved, their neighbors brought food and carried away tidbits of conversation. Days later a schoolmate remembered Mary had talked of an invitation to tea and cookies at the Lodge. Mr. Sullivan and four parishioners raced to the Lodge, but found the doors locked and cobwebs draping the barred windows. Everyone talked of brave Mary Sullivan, a credit to her name, but the locals walked on the opposite sidewalk when they passed the Lodge. ◊

THE PEARL CHAIN
D.K. McCUTCHEN

An MFA grad at the University of Massachusetts, D.K. McCutchen has stories forthcoming in Hayden's Ferry Review *and* Rosebud Literary Magazine *as well as a number of nonfiction publications in newspapers and science magazines.* The Whale Road, *a full-length manuscript, recently made finalist in* The Bellwether Awards, *won a Boscov Scholarship, and a Money for Women, Barbara Demming Memorial grant. Excerpts won a Faulkner Award, honorary mention in the AWP Journals Project, and first place in a FRESCH! online short story award.*

She'd had a lover once, but he had died. It was the tragedy that invested her life with meaning. Gave her every sigh depth. Lent her footsteps their measured tread.

She had loved him with a perfect, avaricious love, one which memorized every gesture of her chosen, every nuance of speech and flick of his surprised brows. She could conjure the cracking of his knuckles, the timber of his voice in its last farewell—as if she'd known he must die.

Some whispered unkindly that death was the only escape for one so loved.

Sorrow was her daylight face, but in the evening she seemed content. As dusk fell she put away her loss with her chores, closing the shutters on her rituals of bereavement. Shut away, she built up the fire, threw upon it certain bitter herbs which burned with a faint musk of dusty streets and sweet, old corpses. She took out her knitting and invoked the memory of her own true love.

Knit one, purl one, and the beloved's face wavered in firelight. Knit one, purl two and slender fingers drummed restlessly on her battered table top. Knit one, purl three and his querulous tenor was asking her again the question it always asked, night after night.

"Why?" The ghost whispered in an upward rush of flame-driven air.

"Whyyyyyyyyyyy?" hissed the gas lantern by her elbow.

"You are my Eternal Love," the woman said aloud in the empty, ghost flickering room.

"I am so tired of this," his cruel last words took her breath away anew and she knitted angrily, his form in the firelight thickening with her fierce concentration.

"You are mine," she said sharply. Knotting her memories furiously into each stitch. Knit one, purl one....

"Let me go," the ghost whined around the window, fingers drumming.

She hears it every night, conjures the pain and the ghost in her agony of devotion. On this night, the crack of a gas pocket ignites in the fireplace like the snap of a door opening, making her look up. She drops a stitch. A great gash appears across the face of her memory. "Aah," the ghost grins too widely.

"No! That's wrong!" She shrieks, tearing at her knitting. As it unravels, the skin of the ghost peels away in long fleshy ropes until only the surprised eyebrows rise over shrunken holes, squirming—twinkling—with an invasion of hopeful worms.

"Oh," sighs her lost love, "yes."

"You...have...no...right...to...go," the woman pants, desperately clutching her raveling skeins. "You have no right!" She screams, plunging knitting needles into knotted threads, slashing—stabbing at him again. (Again.)—until the threads wind around her needles in a parody of fabric or flesh, a thick, clotted ball of tangles.

"You can *not* leave me now," she says, looking upon the face of her love—brown skin, gleaming teeth, and putrid horror—with satisfaction. "I will keep you with me always."

And the ghost howls in fear and pain.... ◊

THE UNFINISHED MUSIC
CHRISTOPHER CONLON

Christopher Conlon has had work in The Washington Post, America Magazine, Tennessee Williams Annual Review, Filmfax, *and many other publications, including the fantasy collection* California Sorcery *(Ace Books), for which he wrote the Introduction, and* September 11, 2001: American Writers Respond *(Etruscan Press). His fiction for* The Long Story *literary journal is available in his book* Saying Secrets *(Writers Club); he is also the author of a poetry chapbook,* What There Is *(Argonne House). A former Peace Corps volunteer, Conlon now lives and works in Silver Spring, Maryland. His website can be accessed at www.christopherconlon.com.*

I

As a woman who has for many years structured her life around pleasant routine and the avoidance of unnecessary disturbance, it was with some irritation that I considered my sister's letter inviting me to visit her and her husband at their home in New England. Irritation—and attendant guilt as well, for after all, I supposed, one should feel gratitude for such thoughtfulness. And yet irritation prevailed, largely because it was an invitation I could not easily decline. I had not seen my sister in over five years—we were never close—and this letter describing the happy benefits of "a few relaxing weeks in the country" was, I knew, the product of careful thought and consideration. My sister had always regretted, much more so than I, the distance between us; and she made these occasional overtures in a transparent attempt to bridge the gap, a gap which did not overmuch concern me.

I do not mean to sound cold. There was a great deal of trauma in our early lives, brought on largely by our father's alcoholism and the inability of our mother to stand as an equal to him. There was no physical violence toward us; instead there was what I believe the TV show psychiatrists now refer to as "psychological violence." We were constantly pitted against each other, compared with each other, usually with Anne—my sister, two years younger than myself—having the better of it. Anne had the kind of personality usually described as "bubbly," and she was liked by both our parents. I, however, was not bubbly, and was generally considered dull and bookish. The friction this caused between my sister and myself is of a predictable nature, and yet the fact that it had carried all the way over into our thirties is perhaps testament to the tenacity with which our father set out, over many years, to ensure our estrangement. The auto accident which had taken both our parents' lives a decade before had done nothing to bring us closer. The patterns are, as is well known today, difficult to break. Indeed, I have had my own periodic bouts with my father's affliction, and this also contributed, over the years, to the distance between Anne and myself.

But to blame the entire situation entirely on our parents would be disingenuous. Generally speaking, I did not *want* to be closer to my sister. She had her own life with her husband, and had become a happy homemaker with as little apparent ambition as housewives of generations before. I, in contrast, enjoyed my career at the university, teaching Music History along with Critical Theory to our more scholarly graduates and undergraduates—preparing them for careers in the academic end of music, as professors and researchers and critics. I took enormous pleasure in the fact that one of my books (on the Romanticism of Stravinsky, Berg, and Bartok) was a required text in advanced Music courses throughout the country. I enjoyed the recognition on the campus in Oklahoma, the respect of my colleagues—and I enjoyed, though perhaps reluctant to admit it, being called "Doctor Graver." At the age of thirty-five, then, living in the Midwest and focusing on my burgeoning career, I had little in common with my sister and little reason to wish to see her again, other than for the opportunity to relive painful memories I had spent fifteen years trying to forget.

After a week of indecision, however—and quietly seeking a way to say no without being abjectly rude about it—I bowed to the inevitable and accepted the invitation. It was late summer, turning toward autumn; as I was on a working sabbatical, finishing a book on the textual problems of Mahler's uncompleted Tenth Symphony, I would have no classes again until January. With a sense of resignation I packed two bags—one with personal items, the other with books, music scores, and manuscripts—and began the two-day drive to New England.

I had not been to their home before—they had purchased it only the previous year—and as I drove up a long, winding path of gravel toward it, I was not favorably impressed. It was a rather moldering old Colonial typical of the backroads of New England, thought of by many as charmingly rustic but by myself as grandiose and forbidding: its marble pillars belonged not to a home but to a cold, echoing museum. I have never liked such houses. A simple, unpretentious structure, with a decent lawn and garden and many sun-warmed windows, like my own home, seemed to me more suitable for human habitation than this kind of aged monstrosity with its creaking boards and faulty wiring. Still, the setting was undeniably majestic—on a gentle slope, surrounded on all sides by the wonderfully various foliage of New England, the falling leaves like sparks of fire, the damp earth, the wind rustling and murmuring in the trees; and thus my mood was, if not actually happy, then at least at ease as I stepped from the car and made my way up the front walk to the imposing oak doors.

Anne pulled them open before I could knock; and threw her arms around me. "Dolly!" she cried. "How wonderful that you've come!"

She looked well. Obviously matrimony and country living agreed with her. Her blue eyes sparkled with radiance, her cheeks glowed with vitality; her whole being was suffused with a healthy radiance. She wore blue jeans and a lavender blouse tied at the midriff. I smiled as we exchanged the usual small talk: the drive, the weather. She showed me into the sitting room, an opulent, high-ceilinged affair decorated in pleasant earth tones, and we chatted lightly. It was late afternoon; as I was tired from the journey, we agreed that we would take an early supper as soon as her husband arrived and I would go to bed early.

The conversation between us followed predictable routes, with numerous silences. Her life, their plans for the house; my life, my career. Anne was bouncy, animated; she served tea as we watched the sun slowly drop behind the mountain which we could see from the front room.

"I do have some good news," Anne said at last, her face beaming.

"Yes?"

"Well," she began, "I wasn't going to tell you this until after Ben came home, but—oh, Dolly, I'm going to have a baby!"

This news was greeted as if on cue by the arrival of her husband, Ben Bright, a boisterous, heavy-set man with a large walrus mustache. I had met him only once, at their wedding, and I remembered thinking him a pleasant-enough fellow. We shared an occupation, for he taught Biology at a nearby university. He too seemed happy and healthy and greeted me with a kiss on the cheek and a hearty, unabashedly corny rendition of the first verse of "Hello, Dolly." We all laughed.

"I've heard the good news," I said. "Congratulations."

"Oh yes," Ben said, going to Anne and putting a big affectionate arm around her. "It appears that all our hard work and sacrifice have paid off at last."

Anne laughed. "What sacrifice was that, Ben?"

"Well, missing most of the Mets' night games, for one thing."

Laughter all around again. Ben and my sister kissed playfully and finally, after what seemed a very long time, we went to the dining room for supper.

I was unaccountably depressed when I went to bed. Nothing had happened in the ensuing hours to justify this; and I was annoyed with myself. I lay in the white-covered bed—it was like a bed of snow—and stared at the old-fashioned ceiling fan above me, still and silent in the darkness. The house was exceedingly quiet. From where I lay I could see the window at the other side of the room: the two lacy white curtains, the rectangle of blackness they framed. I fidgeted, tossed from side to side. I am not accustomed to sleeping in strange beds.

After a time I sat up and listened to the silence—but it was not, I realized slowly, silence.

There was a sound—soft, muffled—persistent but unidentifiable. It was rather like a softly muffled heartbeat; and for a moment I wondered if it was my own heart. But no: the sound was coming from somewhere else. I tried to place it but could not; it seemed, however, oddly omnipresent, the way a cricket's chirping is in a summer dark. Listening, I realized that it was not steady. Its rhythm was erratic.

Thump. Thump thump. Thump.

Two beats might be followed by one, or three, or none at all. There was no pattern to it. The unevenness of the sound made me more curious and finally I stood and walked to the window. I listened, thinking that it most likely came from outside. I opened the window and was met with a gust of cold air whipping my face. I listened to the dark for some time: but there was nothing.

Closing the window, I turned again to the dim room. The sound continued its uneven tattoo: thump thump. Thump thump thump. Thump. It was a soft sound, not loud, not harsh or even bothersome: merely curious: indeed, when I walked across the carpet again toward the bed, my own footsteps drowned it out. The sound was nearly indistinguishable from the silence.

And yet when I was in bed again it came back to me. I listened, my emotions unidentifiable and strange. There was something entrancing in the sound, like a hypnotist's sleepy drone. I listened for a long time in the darkness, until the gentle beating carried me away into a soft sleep.

"D̲o you have problems with the pipes here, Anne?"
We were on the verandah, looking out upon her lush garden of flowers, while we breakfasted on fresh fruit and tea. The sky was icily clear.

"The pipes?" She looked at me blankly. "No, I don't think so. Why?"

I leaned back in my chair, sinking my hands deeply into the pockets of my sweater and staring absently at the music manuscripts piled on the chair between us. "Oh, it's nothing," I said. "Just a bit of noise last night. Some kind of thumping sound."

"Well, old houses like this, you know..."

"Mm-hm."

"They have a lot of creaks and strange noises." She smiled. "Ben's inheritance bought us a pretty nice house, but not a *perfect* one. Did it keep you awake?"

"No, no, only for a few minutes."

"Oh, I'm sorry."

It was silly, this elaborate courtesy between us; but such was our relationship. Anne looked very well that morning—her blonde hair fresh and windblown, her blue blouse and sweater and jeans appealingly simple. My younger sister was, I realized, a very attractive woman: no more so than here, where she seemed to have bloomed in this wifely country life. When she spoke, when she moved, it was with utter, carefree confidence. I had never seen her so happy.

After breakfast I asked to be left alone for an hour or two in order to make a few sketches for my next chapter in Mahler. Anne cheerfully agreed: "It's such a nice morning for work. You could get a lot done here if you would decide to stay awhile."

"School does beckon," I said, returning the smile.

"But you've got months. You told us last night. Why not finish your book here?"

"I don't know, Anne. You may get sick of me. Anyway, I do still have responsibilities at the university, sabbatical or not. I still meet with the Ph.D. candidates and I still help some of the Master's students with their theses. I'm a busy girl, really."

Anne smiled down at me, dishes in her hand. "What's this one about? Your book, I mean."

"Mahler's Tenth Symphony."

She looked at me blankly. "Oh."

"It's very interesting, actually," I said. "Mahler was working on it when he died. He had completed it in—" I did not want to get too technical—"in what's called the short score, that is, without orchestration. In other words, we have the music, the *notes,* but except for the first movement we don't know how the music is supposed to be played, or by what instruments. Different people have tried finishing it over the years. My book is about that—the symphony's history, first of all, then the different positives and negatives of the later orchestrations."

"Do you still play, Dolly?" she asked me.

I smiled, looking down. "You have a long memory, Anne."

"You used to play so *beautifully,"* she said. "I can still remember how the sound of that cello used to fill the house."

I chuckled. "It wasn't that good. I really wasn't much of a cellist."

"You were."

"Well, anyway," I said, "no. I still own one. I fool around on it now and then. But I haven't kept up. Life is too crowded."

There was a brief pause. "Just let me put these things away," Anne said finally, moving into the house. "You go ahead with your work."

"Thank you, Anne." I watched her move away, thinking unpleasantly of the cello which leaned against the wall of my bedroom back in Oklahoma. Occasionally I would wipe the dust away with a soft cloth; once in a long while I would position myself on the edge of my bed, take up my bow, and draw it slowly across the strings. In truth, I was an adequate cellist and was now and then requested to fill in a slot in a faculty quartet. But I never much enjoyed it anymore, and avoided it when I could. I do not like doing things at which I cannot excel.

Music history, now: there I knew I was on much firmer

ground. I took up the Mahler manuscript and one of the orchestrations I was reviewing, finding myself absorbed within minutes, studying as the orchestrator attempted to yield up the symphony's secrets—sometimes succeeding, I believed, but more often failing. I had once begun an attempt of my own to orchestrate this work, but my effort lay unfinished. It had been, initially, an exhilarating job; to study a great, dying composer's final manuscript and try to give it orchestrated life was like conversing with the ghost of genius. I remembered that as I had worked I had even begun to mentally address Mahler himself as if he were a mute participant: Now, Gustav, I would think, how did you mean this measure to relate to the theme—darkly, as you've done it a few pages earlier (in which case, perhaps cellos and basses), or more gently and reflectively (woodwinds)? Tell me and I will bring it to life just as you would have done.

But ultimately I found that I could not conjure Mahler's ghost—not consistently, at least—and somewhere early in the fourth movement I abandoned my effort. Still, the experience had ignited a curious interest in me, one that over the past three years had developed into something of a specialty of mine: the study of unfinished music. To some in the department, it seemed a strange preoccupation. But I found it fascinating, to pour over these scores and attempt to divine through close analysis the composer's final, fading thoughts. Mahler's unfinished Tenth Symphony is only one example; the musical woods are filled with them—Puccini's *Turnadot,* Berg's *Lulu;* Bruckner's Ninth Symphony, Elgar's Third, Beethoven's Tenth (a few sketches for a first movement); Bach's *Art of the Fugue;* Mozart's *Requiem Mass.* I had already completed my study of the Bruckner; I planned monographs on all the rest. I spent most of the next hour in satisfied contemplation of the Mahler, frequently consulting alternate orchestrations, sometimes checking one of the earlier Mahler scores I had brought with me for comparison.

But I found slowly growing within me a sense of disquiet, and I broke off from my work earlier than I had anticipated. Something curious had begun to happen as I studied the notes. I began to hear a soft beating inside my mind, so vivid that I thought for a moment it was something actually indicated in the score— the last movement, for instance, which opens with the slow beating of a funeral drum. I realized soon enough, however, that it was inside my own skull. I thought briefly that it was a headache, but it was not pulsing in time with my heart as my headaches always do. The beating had, in fact, no rhythm at all: and I suddenly became aware that I was hearing the beating from last night again. It was replaying in my memory like a remembered passage of music, insistently repetitious. It was not the beating itself, I was sure of that; instead it was my remembrance of it, exactly like the numerous times I would have a brief passage—often no more than a few notes—of a piece of music stuck in my head, usually from the cello repertoire, often Brahms or Dvorak. I leaned closer to the notes I had been studying, conjuring them into sound in my mind in an attempt to silence the strange, halting *Thump. Thump thump thump. Thump thump.* But after a few moments I knew that this would not succeed; and, what was more, I found that I did not want it to. The beating was in no way unpleasant; it was a soft, rather soothing sound, like the sea or a distant foghorn. It was very strange, the fact that I could not dislodge it from my mind; but, I reasoned, it must have continued after I had fallen asleep the night before, and made an impression on my unconscious. Strange too was the effect the soft tattoo had on my emotions: I felt suddenly becalmed, free of anxieties or concerns. I sat on the early-autumn verandah, a cool breeze drifting through the blazing trees, listening to the soft beating inside my mind; blissfully unaware of the disaster that, even then, was rushing to meet me.

2

That night the sound began almost immediately after my head touched the pillow. I sat upright, holding the sheets close to me. What I felt was not fear, but rather the inexorable sensation of something about to happen. I was not afraid of the sound; it was as soft and pleasant as the night before; but now I was convinced that it was something more than aged pipes. How I knew this I cannot say; it is one of a number of unanswerable questions which occur to me now, after the fact. Why did the sound, which after all was nothing in itself—hardly noticeable—so entrance me? Why did I not ask my sister or her husband to investigate where it came from? And why did I never search out the sound in the daylight, after the morning sun had risen, when logic and reason might have prevailed? I have no response. I can, however, recall—indeed, cannot forget—the peculiar dream-like state of mind which transfixed me each time I heard the soft beating in the darkness. I felt as if I had found myself within the kind of dream in which the dreamer realizes what is happening is not real: that he is in fact in bed, asleep. This was a similar sensation, but oddly reversed; that is, although it *felt* like the dream state, I knew that in fact I was *not* dreaming. A part of me stood as if outside myself, looking at the scene dispassionately, and this part of me knew with absolute certainty that what was happening was in every sense real.

Sitting up in bed, the snow-white sheets bundled around me, I listened closely to the soft *Thump thump thump. Thump. Thump.* I strained to find the direction from which the sound came and discovered, after several minutes of intense concentration, that it seemed to emanate from behind the closet door.

After staring at the door uncertainly for a long moment, I felt again the waves of peace that washed over me with the sound: and I stood, wrapped my robe around me, and moved to the closet in the darkness. I pulled open the door softly. There was a three-quarter moon that night, I recall, and its silvery light streamed into the recesses of the closet in a nearly electric sheen. Inside the closet was something I now remembered having seen before, though it had made no impression on my memory: a small metal trunk, smooth and colorless, was placed neatly in a far corner. Otherwise, with the exception of my own things, the closet was empty. I leaned down and pulled the trunk toward me. It looked to be relatively new, placed there most likely by Anne or Ben after moving here. It was free of dust, undented, with a shiny silver clasp over its front. I leaned my head toward the trunk and had the impression that the beating came from within it.

My sensation of utter peace combined now with curiosity, I unclasped the case and opened it.

Inside the trunk was the kind of paraphernalia one would expect of a Biology teacher. Test tubes, beakers, the disassembled parts of a microscope, devices for clasping and stirring—so it was Ben's; and I felt a vague sense of disappointment, somehow, though I had yet to solve the mystery of the beating, which, when I stopped to listen, still continued. I rummaged through the various pieces of glass and metal, not knowing what I was looking for, until at the very bottom of the case I found something whose sudden appearance caused me to start.

Within a medium-sized glass jar, floating in a clear solution, was a human infant. Its skin was moon-pale, the color of plants grown entirely in darkness. Its limbs, tiny and only partially formed, with fingers no more than slightly protrudent from the hands and no toes at all, resembled fragile flippers. The face, eyeless, with only two small holes where the nose should have been, seemed an expressionless mask. The entire small body, as soft and spongy as it appeared to be, gave the impression of being wholly boneless; it was difficult to imagine anything as solid as bone within such an apparently malleable and clay-like skin. This impression was no doubt incorrect. But as I stared at the long-dead child, a boy, floating in its womb of chemicals for pickling and preserving, I found the idea hard to shake: the body seemed entirely free of hard angles, whether at the jaws, elbows, or anywhere else—instead it was composed of gently undulating curves that led softly from head to shoulders, chest to legs and feet.

I pulled back from my gazing and moved my eyes from the jar. It occurred to me, distantly, that I still had not found the source of the beating sound; but the sound had, since I had found the jar, abruptly ceased. I put the scientific paraphernalia back into the trunk, latched the clasp, and pushed the trunk to the rear of the closet again. I closed the closet door and returned to my bed.

The room was for some time silent. I found myself drifting off into sleep, fragments of past images flickering by in my darkening mind: my father shouting drunkenly at me and hurling aside a book I had been reading; drawing my bow across my cello at a recital when I was thirteen—completing the Brahms Sonata in E Minor, with my music instructor at the piano, all but flawlessly to an audience of parents which did not include my father; years later, a man's face, a man whom I briefly loved but who shared my own affliction, the affliction of my father; and the result of that love, clenching my stomach in the darkness, my entire being suddenly emptied of the life-spark it had, until that afternoon, contained, my body filled now only with shadows.

As I drifted, consciousness fragmenting and sinking into sleep, I became aware once again of the soft tattoo in the room. It did not startle me. Instead, it played as if it were a natural rhythmic accompaniment to the pictures and sounds floating in my mind. I am convinced now that I was in some sort of hypnotic state. In any event, with my mind loosened by its partial unconsciousness, I soon found strange ideas flowing across it. I had not found the source of the beating; but my mind thought again of the spongy biology specimen in the jar, floating senselessly in its poison womb.

I thought (and if this sounds insane I must say again that my mental state was not entirely conscious, and what consciousness I did have seems in retrospect drugged or entranced): What if that infant—through some fantastic, inexplicable mechanism beyond human understanding—were not actually dead?

What, I wondered, if it had some semblance of life—or, if not precisely life, at least some semi-awareness, some level of consciousness, and it realized, at least on a blindly instinctive level, that it was not where it belonged? What if...And here I recall feeling sharply conscious, very much awake: What if it were attempting to escape?

I listened to the thumping, feeling the darkness around me. I opened my eyes, thinking the idea would drift off in a sanity of wakefulness, and yet it did not. The sound continued, gently but insistently, as it had since I first turned out the light in this room the night before. I found myself posing a question inside my mind: What would it sound like, I asked myself, if one put a glass jar filled with a small body and preserving solution into a metal trunk, closed it, put it in the back of a closet and then closed the door? There would be no sound, I knew, for there was nothing to produce it. But what would it sound like—again I asked myself—if, through some process as yet unknown, the body within the jar had in fact some consciousness, even a limited mobility, and it began shaking, in an effort to escape, the wall of its cylindrical prison, causing the jar to bump softly against the side of the trunk?

I could not escape the conclusion. It would sound, I knew, exactly like the soft tattoo which even now was beating gently within the room.

The resilience of the human mind is a wondrous thing. It has an endless grab-bag of tricks with which to handle extreme circumstances. The TV talk show psychiatrists often trot out the evidence: women with dozens of personalities, for instance, which their minds create for them to escape abuse or neglect; or, within darker corridors, psychopaths who cope with their feelings of inadequacy and rage through serial murder. Both are strategies by which the mind deals with the intolerable. So it was, perhaps, with myself. No, I neither created additional personalities nor resorted to murder. Instead, my mind dealt with the apparent reality of a pale, bloodless, long-dead infant's inexplicable animation by handling it simply as an everyday reality. I do not think there is anything unusual in this. Soldiers in combat, for instance, learn to face unspeakable horror and treat it as humdrum. There is, of course, an element of denial in it: but with that denial, one copes. In addition, in my own case, I had the strange entranced sensation which I at all times felt when hearing the soft beating, the feeling that, though real, reality had become a dream.

I had not had a drink in nearly two years and I have never been prone to hallucinations of sight or sound; perhaps this too contributed to my unthinking acceptance of the idea that the child in the jar had become animate. In any event, as I lay in the darkness of the room listening, I grew quickly to complete conviction that the baby in the glass was in some form alive. At the same time, the trance-like state I found myself in did not allow for the kind of quick action one might imagine. Instead I lay there, staring into the darkness as the peaceful sound of the beating washed over me, calming me, soothing me with its pleasant waves. It was beyond my capacity at that moment to consider logical questions. I lay on the bed, serenely contemplating the soft beating.

At last I stood and moved again to the closet door and opened it. I brought out the trunk again and removed the miscellaneous items; then, crouched there, I took the jar in my hands and held it up to the moonlight. It was less weighty than I might have imagined. I studied the pale form within the solution closely, searching for any sign of movement or recognition; but I found none. At last I placed the jar on the floor and watched as the still form bumped and swayed into motionlessness again.

I at no time questioned the reality of the child's new existence. Instead I felt—what did I feel?

I tapped on the glass, very softly. The tiny body drifted.

I tapped again.

I studied the child's ghostly, immature features: the nose and ears which had not yet developed; the stub-fingers, like buds just beginning their fragile rise through the earth; the smooth shapeless chest and belly. If it had moved then, if I had seen its flapper-arms suddenly begin to wave or its tiny mouth-slit open, I would not have been surprised or afraid. But it did not move. Still: the conviction had materialized unalterably within me that the child was not dead—at least, not dead in the way that I knew death. I gazed closely at the moon-flesh.

Little frog, I thought in the silvery darkness, *your name must be Putzi.*

It took me a moment to think where my mind had conjured such a peculiar appellation. I imagined for a moment that it was a name my father had used for me, but he had never called me by a pet-name; and it occurred to me finally that "Putzi" was the name Mahler had used for his beloved first daughter Maria, who died of scarlet fever before her fifth birthday. *Each morning,* the composer's widow wrote, *Putzi would go into Mahler's study where they had long talks. Nobody has ever known what about.*

Putzi, I thought, looking at the softly floating form.

And as I repeated the name in my mind I saw—I believed that I saw—a tiny, almost imperceptible movement within the glass jar. It could have been a trick of the light but I did not think so: no, one of the feeble flipper-arms had seemed in fact to move, to swing definitely to one side, and the fluid in the jar seemed to jostle very slightly. I placed my face near the glass, only inches from the infant inside. The moon-glow poured through the liquid, giving him a silver sheen. I studied the little body for what must have been a very long time, but I did not detect any further animation. He was still again.

It occurred to me after a time that the room was not as dark as it had been, that the silver sheen was fading; and, looking up, I realized that the first hints of dawn were beginning to glow through the window frame. Instinctively—I cannot explain how I knew to do this—I took the jar and placed it back into the trunk, put the other laboratory pieces inside in approximately the positions they had previously occupied, and after a final look at the tiny form my mind had christened Putzi, closed the case and returned it to its position in the closet. I closed the closet door. Then I collapsed onto the bed, a sudden wave of utter exhaustion overcoming me. Behind my closed eyes came a faint orange light, the coming of day. The room was absolutely silent.

I arose past noon. Anne could not resist a playful remark about how relaxing I was obviously finding the pure country air, and how indicative it was of the fact that I should plan for a long visit. Sitting out on the verandah for lunch, a cool breeze wafting through the woods, Anne spoke of the change of seasons, of "putting the garden to bed" because of the cold as well as the fact that she would be less active in the coming months.

"Why is that, Anne?" I asked absently.

"The baby, of course," she said. "I'll try to stay as busy as I can, but I'm sure I'll have to slow down."

Absurdly, I had for a moment thought she was referring to

my experience of the night before. Had it happened? I wondered. Obviously it had not. I felt fully normal. That was the problem: the trance-state which I recalled from the night before, the soft waves of peace, were now wholly absent—and I felt rather as if I had just come off a prolonged bout with the affliction of my father. My mood was black. Reality seemed vacant and colorless and it was not for some time that I even realized a clean blue sky was shining down upon us. I had mentally assumed the skies were misty and gray, for when I stepped outside they had seemed that way to me. Had it all been one fantastically prolonged dream? Had I been sleepwalking? Had some mysterious element in the food the day before poisoned me, leading me into a temporary delirium? I could only hope that one of these explanations was true; for the alternative was too ghastly to contemplate. I could, I realized, be going mad.

I moved mentally back through the day before and tried to remember if I had touched any alcohol at all, at any time, in any quantity. That could be an explanation. But there had been nothing, not so much as a sip of wine, and for all the deranged intensity of my worst bouts, I could always remember, later, the drinking that had induced them. I did not know the explanation. I also could not comprehend, given the absence of alcohol, my despairing mood: for it felt exactly like one of the awful hangovers I would have after two or three days of haze. My head, my entire body ached; I could feel my heart beating malevolently behind my eyes. I was exhausted. My body felt heavy and sluggish, as if I had suddenly gained a tremendous amount of weight. But worst of all was the overhanging sensation of *gloom*: it infected everything, the meal, the leaves, the floating forest odors: they all seemed dull, tasteless and colorless and odorless.

But I could remember—still, vividly!—the sensations of the fever-dream. How alive I had felt! How aware I had been of every sensation, every sound, every tone of the moonlit night. That was no doubt typical, I thought, of whatever fever or poison that had had control of my being. And yet I found myself missing it sorely, that sense of super-heightened awareness, sensation: the feeling that this is real, this is *happening*. In contrast, the table before me, my sister and the trees beyond, seemed mere shadows.

I attempted to work in the afternoon, but my senses were too dull to follow the reams of curly-cues and doodles I was trying to analyze. In order to study music I must be able to hear it inside my own mind, to translate the black streaks and dots into the sound of instruments and voices. I found no such concentration available to me that day. Instead there was grayness and an accompanying anxiety. I tried to forget all of it, to shuck it off like a useless skin. Anne took me for a drive that day, late in the afternoon as the sun sank low behind the mountains; but the appeal of the landmarks and natural beauty to which she pointed were lost on me. An historic house, tree groves or hills: it was all dully the same, and my mood remained unchanged.

When we returned, I told Anne that I needed to nap for a time; I would be down for dinner. But when I began to ascend the stairs toward the room I had been using, something stopped me. I felt a tinge of fear, as if my madness—if I were indeed going mad—was waiting for me somewhere within those four walls. Instead, I stepped gingerly back down the stairs and lay out on the sofa in the main room.

I closed my eyes, but again fear assailed me. If what had happened was some kind of dream or hallucination, was it safe to fall asleep again? Would I find the visions once again overwhelming me? The scene had been so vivid the night before; so breathlessly real; if it were the result of fever, might not the fever return?

And what (I wondered, my eyes closed against the twilight)

if it did? The world I had experienced the night before, the calm serenity, was very different from any world I had ever known. Perhaps I was making too much of this. After all, if it was merely a fabulously rich dream, what was the harm in a dream? I could remember from years before, when I was a girl, dreams of strong arms and masculine odors entwining me: the dreams had been more, ultimately, than the reality, and they had left much more pleasant memories. But dreams could, I knew, twist suddenly. Years before, for months after I last saw the man I had loved who shared my affliction (his red, shouting face as I bolted down the stairs after the disaster) I had a dream of the three of us, he and myself and the baby who was not to be, in a close-knit, happy family embrace; but when I looked up at my dream-husband's face the skin suddenly melted away leaving a screaming skull, and when I tried to bundle the baby in my arms to flee I looked down to discover that the blankets I held were empty.

Memories of this dream frightened me into remaining awake, breathing evenly, not betraying myself when Anne entered the room and covered me with a wool blanket.

I began to hear snatches of music inside my head, a fragment of the Brahms Sonata in E Minor, a tender moment from the Dvorak Cello Concerto; and then I heard the slow, funereal beats of the muffled drum which open the final movement of Mahler's Tenth Symphony. *Only you know what it means,* the composer had written to his wife in the margin of the score, a reference to a day when, from their hotel room over New York's Central Park, they had heard a low, somber drumbeat, and Mahler, opening the window, had witnessed a huge public funeral procession moving down the street. Deeply moved, he had incorporated the sound into his final, unfinished symphony. It is a haunting effect, but is always played too harshly and rapidly in orchestrated performances; no one—not Mazetti, not Wheeler, not Deryck

Cooke in either of his editions—has captured it correctly. Clinton Carpenter came the nearest, but his work is otherwise dreadful. My own orchestration, I knew, would at last solve all the problems, finally opening this most profound of all moments in Mahler to listeners everywhere.

Then I remembered that I had abandoned my orchestration. The task had simply been too large and emotionally draining for me to complete. It did not seem too large now, lying here in the dimness; but I knew that reality had a way of wearing one down, day after day, year after year, and that those Herculean tasks we think we can accomplish when we are half-asleep are a thousand times more daunting in the cold light of day. I felt suddenly that I did not much like day. I liked night: I liked peace, I liked an absence of commitments, I liked extended communion with myself. I was slipping into sleep. A picture of Mahler brushed across my mind as fragments of the Tenth Symphony wound through me. I saw a cello propped in a corner. I heard myself saying *Daddy, don't*. Then a voiced name wove into the fabric of the music I heard: whispered by someone I did not know, it repeated softly, over and over: Putzi. Putzi.

3

The free-flowing, softly ecstatic sensation of the previous night again poured over me, exactly as before, after I had gone to bed. A glass of wine at dinner, just one, had calmed my anxieties and convinced me that I was being foolish in my fear of the bedroom. Surely I had simply had some touch of food poisoning or a virus of some kind. But, literally moments after I had switched out the light and lay down, the tattoo began again.

Logic would have it that I should have been instantly terrified; here was my fever, or madness, come back again. But I felt no fear whatsoever. Again the feeling of smooth serenity washed over my mind and it was much the most pleasant sound in the world, that soft beating; for I knew now where it came from, and why. After a few minutes of deep, calm breathing and relaxation in the quiet pulses of sound, I stood and moved toward the closet.

Putzi was there, luminous in the dark night, and I studied his soft features for a long while as he drifted inside the jar. Putzi, I wondered, why do you stop moving every time I come close to you? Are you shy? Afraid? It made sense, I realized. After all, his first stab at life had led someone to place him in a grotesque pickling jar for the gawking study of undergraduates. It was no wonder he was afraid to make his animation known.

I understand, Putzi, I thought to myself. Somehow I was sure the thought was communicating itself to him.

I decided to treat him like a shy kitten. I would leave him where he was, and he could come out toward me when he chose. Pushing the other instruments out of the way, I placed the jar back into the comforting darkness of the trunk; but I tilted the trunk on its side, so that the bottom of the jar was now only a fraction of an inch from the floor. I was about to move away when I looked again at the jar and realized, seeing the infant's sadly underformed limbs, that it could never have the strength to escape such a tightly-lidded prison.

I loosened the lid, unscrewing it quietly and leaving it unattached on the top of the jar. I detected a sour odor of chemicals.

I made my way back to my bed and lay there, waiting.

I never doubted that he would come; and with my serene mood controlling all my thoughts, it did not surprise me when I heard the soft clatter of the lid striking the floor.

I waited. I did not look.

After some time I heard vague watery sounds, like a small body thrashing weakly within liquid. I wanted to stand, to help; but I knew I would frighten him back into his false stillness. I waited, not moving a muscle. The room was very quiet and I missed the sound of the soft beating; but when I heard the sounds of water being displaced, my sadness was replaced by an ecstatic excitement.

At last there was a small *thud.*

How I wanted to look; how I had to strain to keep my head from whipping to its side to see what I knew would be there! But I did not move. I stayed utterly still, my body completely motionless but for my chest slowly rising and falling.

There was the sound of something dragging along the carpet of the room. A small thing, hardly audible, it moved very slowly. I realized how very weak he must be. How many years had he waited inside the jar?

Then, very slowly, almost imperceptibly, I moved my arm down toward the floor, leaving my fingers passively limp. After a long time I sensed that the motion below me had stopped; and then I felt the wet cheek brush again my knuckles, the sensation like a puppy's wet nose. The cheek pulled away; then a soft stubbiness touched my palm. His skin was slimy and cold and this filled me with sorrow; but such feelings vanished as the other stub-hand sought my own and began, very weakly, to tug.

I wrapped my fingers gently around him—he was so small, so terribly small that I could lift him with one hand—and slowly lifted. He did not cry; there was no sound at all. I brought him into my range of vision.

He was even more poignantly beautiful now, freed from the chemicals and the glass. His skin was softer than any baby's. His movements were woefully weak and disoriented. He was blind, I realized; and I wondered if he had been born that way or if—the thought was horrid—someone had undertaken, after his "death," to remove the eyes from their sockets. In any event, there was nothing but flat emptiness behind the closed lids. He shook himself weakly, drops of the glistening chemicals landing on my nightgown. I held him gently in both my hands as he shone in the moonlight. Finally I placed him on my stomach and reached for a hand towel which was on the nightstand. I wiped down his body, the unnatural sheen fading as I did so and leaving a pale, powdered look. The body was very cold and I used part of my blanket as a wrap which I placed loosely around him. As the warm cotton surrounded his shoulders I believe I saw his tiny mouth curve into a smile.

The feeling I had, holding the impossible infant Putzi in my arms, is all but indescribable. Certainly I loved him, with a love surging throughout my body like a ferocious tidal wave. Added to this was a poignancy, a feeling of a thing recovered, a sorrow redeemed, two lost people finding comfort in each other's arms. Questions of science or logic did not enter my mind. All I thought of was Putzi, my soft pale Putzi, as he weakly waved his flipper-arms and opened and closed his little slit of a mouth.

After some time the body seemed to grow at least slightly warmer—though still much colder than any normal infant's skin could ever be—and Putzi began to move more energetically, waving and even beginning to kick. He seemed to want to wander, so I loosened the blanket still further and held him only tightly enough to ensure he would not fall. Blindly the flipper-arms began to push at my stomach; then, eyelessly, he began to move— as if by instinct—up my body until he located my breasts. He began to push softly at them. I opened my nightgown and his cool mouth sought my nipple, sucking with surprising strength: and, although I knew there was no nourishment to be had from them, I nonetheless felt that the baby was deriving something, perhaps as simple as warmth or strength, from the suckling. He seemed, over long minutes, to grow warmer still. Once he raised his head, blindly faced me; and the look on his face was one of utter contentment.

Putzi, I thought. His head tilted up toward me.

You understand me, don't you? You understand what

I'm thinking.

He went back to his suckling, burrowing his little hands as deeply as he could into my flesh.

Putzi, I thought, we will stay together forever. We will have these private times and talks and nobody ever needs to know what they are about.

We remained like that for many hours, Putzi alternately suckling and sleeping—if it could be called sleep. He did not breathe, he had no eyes to close; but he would settle onto my chest and become all but motionless, just the stub-fingers instinctively kneading my skin until, after a long while, he would wake again and start to suckle once more. They were the happiest hours of my life. I have never felt so utterly free of cares, and yet so terribly *needed*. Putzi was mine in a way no other baby could ever be, given my useless womb; but even if I could give birth, I thought, the child would never be mine as this one was. I had not simply given him life. I had *returned* life to him, life which he had known only momentarily before being hurled into the darkness of glass-walled nonexistence. How long would he have been trapped there, I wondered, if I had not answered his tattoo-cry for help? How many undergraduates would have gawked obscenely at his helpless body? When would he have at last sensed the presence of someone he could trust, as he had trusted me?

But inevitably these paradisiacal hours drew to a close, and I felt a pang of grief as I realized that the moon-glow in the room was beginning to fade.

My sweet Putzi, I thought. What can I do with you?

And suddenly I knew: secreting Putzi away, I would leave my sister's house as soon as possible. But I could not simply run—as I so wanted to even now, with the beautiful moon-child in my arms; I could not arouse suspicion. Certainly I did not want to give either of them any reason to want to come look into this room. And Ben must be kept, at all costs, from looking into his trunk. That must not happen for weeks, preferably months; so that when he finally discovered the missing infant, there would be no connection to me.

I knew certain things. I knew that as Mahler's Putzi had been his daughter of morning, mine was a child of night. I did not know what would happen if my Putzi were exposed to the day but I knew—somehow I knew—that it would be catastrophic. The mood, after all, the perfect serenity we both felt when we were together, could exist only in darkness. And so I would have to be careful. I also knew that under no circumstances could I allow Putzi to be discovered.

At last I arrived at a plan.

Putzi, I thought, I must put you back in the jar.

Putzi immediately began thrashing erratically, kicking my ribs. His mouth opened and closed rapidly.

It's only for today, little one. I have to hide you until I can take us away forever. Then we will go to a place where you never have to be in prison anymore. You'll live with me, in my house. You'll stay in the darkness during the day and then we will have every night together forever and ever. Please, Putzi.

He began to calm. I sensed dissatisfaction but he trusted me: and so, with a sinking feeling of sorrow, I lifted him and kissed him over and over.

Only for one day, sweetheart, I thought. One day and we'll be free.

I thought my heart would break as I moved to place Putzi back in the jar; but he did not struggle, and even seemed to smile as I closed the lid.

Goodnight, my love.

By then Putzi had already resumed his act of motionlessness.

I put the jar back into the deep recess of the trunk and placed everything else over it. I closed up the trunk and shut the closet door.

I'll be back in just a few hours, Putzi, I thought.

But I was not sure, this time, that he heard me.

T he day which broke through the windows of the house was intolerable. Moving downstairs—I had not slept, only dozed intermittently—it struck me how very ugly everything looked in the unforgiving light. Each speck, every dust-mote seemed hugely exaggerated. I glanced at myself in the mirror of the foyer and this redoubled my impression. Dark sacks had appeared under my eyes; my skin was pale and taut, my lips colorless. My mood was one of utter despair.

I made my way into the main room and found a note on the coffee table. *Dear Dolly,* it read, *Sorry I couldn't wait for you to get up but I have a Dr.'s appoint. I'll be back in the afternoon. Ben's at school, back usual time. Feel free to raid the fridge. Love, Anne.* I was alone, then; and I moved to the curtains and pulled them closed, darkening, at least somewhat, the obscene glare of the room. Then I dropped listlessly onto the sofa.

Was it madness? Or was I physically ill? I could recall every detail of last night's phantasm; and yet nothing about it, nothing whatever, seemed the product of imagination. The memories were as real as the sofa beneath me. It seemed, for all the world, to have *happened.* My logical mind, of course, instantly refuted this, and I told myself: Dolly, you are a sick woman. And yet even then, even as I thought it, some deeper part of my mind rebelled. It rebelled in exactly the same way it would have if I had attempted to tell it that the sofa beneath me was not really there, it was just a product of my imagination.

It occurred to me that I could, at least, go upstairs—now, in the sober brightness of day—and look in the closet. But at the same moment I knew that I would not, that the terror of what I might find there, or not find, was too suffocatingly vast to take such a chance. I sat motionless on the sofa. The house was awesomely silent.

At last I could not stand it anymore. I took my handbag and brought out my dark sunglasses. Then I walked out to my car, resolving to go somewhere, anywhere, that would take me away from the house and the soundlessness.

My heart raced as I drove down the winding country road toward the town, storm clouds slowly coming into view overhead. What is happening to me? I thought. I wondered if I should see a doctor; but what I could I possibly say? That I was having a recurring dream of an infant in a jar coming to life? She would prescribe a sedative and tell me to go get some rest. I could no longer discriminate between reality and fantasy. If I could screw up the courage, I thought, to enter the room, to open the closet door and look into the trunk while glaring daylight blazed into the room, I would have my answer: but the thought of finding *nothing* was too terrifying to consider.

Arriving in town, I wasted hours wandering in the few shops. I was simultaneously bored and frightened. Something, I knew, had to happen. I thought of driving on, to the university town twenty miles beyond, but felt too nervous to sit behind the wheel again.

At last I found myself in front of an agreeable-looking lounge. It appeared dark and clean inside: and I resolved to step in, to pass time there until Anne or Ben would be home and I would not be so dreadfully alone. I knew that one glass of wine would not hurt me.

I was correct; the lounge was dim and pleasant, with few patrons at this time of day. I ordered my wine and sat at a corner table. When the wine was delivered I swallowed it greedily; I had never tasted such fine wine. It was truly delicious. The smooth, ripe fluid flowed over my lips and down my parched throat like the waters of the freshest country stream.

Soon the glass was empty. I could handle another. I had done it before; I could stop at two. I ordered it and sat there drinking slowly, methodically, realizing that I had to be careful. It took me quite a time to finish the glass; I had been in the lounge for over an hour. But then I remembered something. Just last year, at the Music Department's Christmas party, I had had three glasses of wine without any side effect. I had stopped, I had gone home, and that was that. So I knew I would be safe if I ordered a third glass.

I did.

When that glass was finished, I began to reason with myself. The difference between three and four, after all, was extremely slight: if I were to drink but one more glass, it would only be one-quarter more than I had already consumed; in other words, three-quarters of my total consumption had already been completed. I convinced myself and ordered a fourth glass.

By the time I returned to my sister's home it was twilight. "Dolly!" Anne cried when she saw me. "Hi! We were beginning to worry!"

I moved into the dining room, where the two of them were in the midst of dinner. "You shouldn't have worried," I said, my tongue slow in my mouth. "I just went shopping. You know."

"Want some dinner?" Ben asked me behind his big mustache, smiling pleasantly.

"No, thank you. I'm not hungry." I dropped into one of the hard dining room chairs.

"And how did you find our little hamlet?" Ben asked, chewing on a pork chop.

"I found it…with great difficulty," I said, a giggle suddenly burbling up inside me.

Ben smiled. Anne looked over at me, scowling thoughtfully.

"Where all did you go, Dolly?" she asked, looking back at her plate again.

"Oh, it was a very cultural experience," I said, my tongue loosening. I was aware that my voice was too loud but I could not seem to quiet myself. "Between the general store on one end and the post office on the other there's a vast cultural world to be explored. The drug store. The dry cleaner's. The pubic—I mean *public*—library. Which even has a couple of dozen books, you know? I was surprised."

Anne put down her fork. "Dolly, have you been drinking?"

"No," I said. "Why do you ask?"

"No reason." She did not look at me.

"Do you think I'm drunk, Anne?" I felt an old rage welling in me.

"I didn't say that."

"I'm *not* drunk."

"I didn't say you were."

"But you don't believe me," I said angrily, feeling the words rushing out. I glanced at Ben. "She's always been like this. Snooping, prying, not trusting her own sister."

"Dolly…" Anne started to say.

"Anyway," I interrupted, standing, "I have some good news for you. I have to leave."

She looked up at me. "Leave? Why?"

"Departmental business," I lied. "They collapse without me, you know. I talked to them on the phone today."

There was silence for a moment. My mind was hazy, disconnected images drifting in and out: Anne, Ben, my father, a pale blind infant.

"Well, we sure wish you wouldn't go," said Ben with false

heartiness, "but if duty calls, duty calls! Tomorrow morning we'll send you off with a real country breakfast."

"Oh," I said, "I'm sorry. You misunderstood. I mean I have to leave now."

Anne looked up again. "Why, Dolly?"

It took me a moment. Finally I gestured toward Ben. "Duty calls," I said. "So if you will excuse me, I will pack and go."

"Dolly," Anne said, standing, "don't. Come on, you're not going anywhere tonight. It's almost dark already."

"Do you think I can't drive in the dark, Anne?"

"That's not what I meant," she said, looking at me with that irritatingly plaintive expression I recognized from many another evening.

"Or do you think I can't drive at all? Is that it?"

She touched the back of a chair absently. "Look, Dolly, just stay here tonight, okay? Then if you still want to go tomorrow, go ahead."

"I am not drunk."

"I never said you were. I never said that."

"It's what you *think,*" I spat, her mincing expression enraging me. "It's what you've always thought."

"Please, Dolly," she said, moving toward me, "don't be upset. I didn't say you were drunk. I just asked you to stay here tonight. I know you don't want to. But please. For us."

"Come on, Dolly," Ben interjected, "you don't want to go out tonight. Looks like it'll rain anyway. Stay here, comfy and cozy."

"I have to leave. I have *commitments—*"

"We know," Anne said, taking my arm. "Just one night. Just stay with us. The roads will be dangerous anyway; they say a big rain is coming."

"I am perfectly capable of driving—"

"Dolly," she said, "for me. For your little sister. Just indulge me. *Please.* I don't want you to get hurt. I love you, Dolly. We both do."

"We do," Ben added. "You bet."

I looked at them through my hazy vision. Night was falling outside and the two of them seemed to become transparent, ghostlike, in the deepening dark. I chuckled derisively at the love-words. What had love ever done for me?

But suddenly, completely without warning, I found myself in tears.

Anne's arms wrapped around me, warm, tight, and she rocked me gently as I wept stupidly and helplessly into her shoulder. "It's all right, Dolly," she whispered, as something hot and sour forced its way through my throat and eyes. "It's all right, Dolly love. It's all right. It's all right."

Nearly all daylight had been extinguished from the windows of the bedroom as Anne helped me onto the bed. I had managed to regain control of myself but still felt weak.

"There you are, sweetheart," Anne chirped. "You're tired. You rest here for the night, get yourself a good night's sleep. Now, where's your nightgown?" She turned toward the closet door.

"Anne…" I tried to say, but my tongue was thick. A great languorousness was beginning to wash over me.

She opened the door; and for a moment I thought that what I saw was an optical illusion. I shook my head, but what I saw remained unchanged.

The trunk was gone. In its place sat only emptiness.

It was possible, I thought—a few cinders of logic rapidly burning out in my brain still feebly glowed—it was possible that there had never *been* a trunk; and if there was no trunk, I was insane; there was no other conclusion.

"Anne..." I said again.

"You hush," my sister said from the closet. "Here, I've found it."

As she moved toward me I forced the words off my slow tongue. "Anne, don't I recall—didn't I see—a trunk in that closet? Before?"

"Oh, yes," she said absently, laying the gown out on the bed. "Ben took it down to the car. It had a bunch of school stuff in it—things for his classes. He's taking it to the university tomorrow."

A feeling of numbness overcame me. I was hardly aware of Anne as she helped take off my clothes and got me into the nightgown. She pushed me gently back onto the bed, tucked the blankets up under my chin. She would make a good mother, I knew.

"Okay now?" she asked, sitting beside me.

I stared at the window opposite. Only the most feeble light shone through now.

"I'm sorry, Anne," I said quietly, my voice hollow and empty. "For everything. I'm...sorry."

I felt her hair on my cheek as she leaned down to embrace me. "You don't have to apologize for anything, Dolly."

"I do."

"Shh."

"I'm scared, Anne."

"There's nothing to be scared of." She looked at me, her eyes only inches from my own. "Nothing at all. You're safe here. You'll always be safe here."

My mouth opened, but for what I wished to say there were no words.

"Time for sleep now," she said at last. She kissed me on the forehead. "If you need anything, Dolly, just give a shout, okay?"

She moved to the doorway, looked back.

"Sweet dreams," she said, and closed the door behind her. I lay breathing in the looming darkness.

Which was more terrifying? I wondered. A trunk that did not exist—or...

But when in a few minutes the light vanished entirely, I felt almost immediately the peaceful waves beginning to sweep over me. All my cares, all the anxieties and fears I had felt during the day were washed smoothly away into silence. All at once I felt unburdened, free. I felt my slow, calm breathing in the velvet dark. It felt so good, then, to be alive—but then I remembered. Putzi: there was no tattoo tonight, no soft beating.

And I knew then that I would have to leave that night. I could wait no longer; tomorrow Putzi would be entirely beyond my reach, floating senselessly in the insulting fluorescent glow of the classroom lights, and Ben would be standing next to him, voice booming out: *Now class, please observe in this specimen the lack of development in*...No: I would not let it happen. I had made a promise to Putzi. We must go, as I had told him we would. Tonight.

I waited for a long time; long after the final lights had been switched off in the other rooms, long after I had heard the sounds of the two of them going to bed. I lay very still.

Putzi? I thought. Can you hear me?

I did not know if he could.

I'm coming, Putzi. I'll be there. Be patient, my love.

Finally, after a long time, I stood and shucked the nightgown, slipping into a blouse and slacks. I pushed my feet into a pair of sandals and then quickly threw my belongings into my suitcase. I tossed the music manuscripts haphazardly into my bag. Then, very quietly, I opened the door.

The hallway was dark and silent. I made my way softly across it and down the stairs. I moved through the rear door which led to the garage.

There, in the back of my brother-in-law's old lime-green sedan, was the trunk. I tried the doors; all four were locked. A sense of panic seized me. I looked around in the dark garage for something, anything: and saw a long, slender strip of wood in a corner. I grabbed it up, frantically thinking of breaking the window somehow, when I noticed that the driver's window was not fully closed—there was a narrow crack between the top of the glass and the door frame. Breathing heavily, I wedged the wood into the crack and created a lever. I worked the window slowly down, several inches, until at last I could reach inside and unlock the door.

I scrambled for the clasp of the trunk, found it, pulled it open. Rummaging quickly through the materials, I at last found the jar and Putzi.

When I saw him, my soul was swept with love and peace. My breathing slowed; my nerves settled.

Hello, my love, I thought. I knew this time he heard me. I looked closely at him floating in the jar.

Time to go home, Putzi, I said within my mind. I saw his little flippers move.

I placed the jar on the garage floor and quietly closed the trunk again. Then I rolled up the window of the car and pushed the door gently closed. I returned the wood strip to the corner where I had found it.

Then I pushed the garage door slowly up; scurrying quickly I threw my bags into the back seat of my car and then returned for Putzi. I carried the jar gingerly across the gravel and placed it on the floor of the passenger seat. Then I returned and gently closed the garage door, noticing the fat raindrops that were beginning to fall.

Returning to the car, I slipped the gearshift into neutral and released the parking brake, pushing the car slowly down the gravel track until the tires met with the main road. Then I pushed it a few yards farther, until my view of the house was obscured by trees. I stepped into the car and fired the engine, slipped into drive and switched on the windshield wipers and headlights. I drove quickly, the black road beginning to glisten with rain.

At last, a few miles from the house, I pulled over and took the jar in my hands. Putzi was there, flipping his tiny arms and legs.

Time to come out, little man. Time to come out and never go back in again.

I unscrewed the lid of the jar. Putzi immediately tried to reach to me. I brought him out of the jar and wiped him down with a blanket which was on the back seat, watching the ugly death-sheen of the chemicals wipe away and his pale powderiness begin to glow again.

Putzi, I thought, holding his little form close to me. Putzi, Putzi, I'll never let them take you back there, we'll be together forever, Putzi.

I opened my blouse and allowed him to suckle for several minutes, his stub-fingers working at my skin. His body warmed quickly. At last, cradling him in one arm, I leaned over and took the jar in my hands.

We won't be needing this anymore, will we, Putzi?

I held him close as I stepped from the vehicle and hurled the jar as far as I could into the bushes. Then I tossed the lid after it.

The rain pelted us coolly. I kissed him over and over, the raindrops splashing onto our faces.

Putzi, I love you, I love you.

I felt tears of emotion stinging my eyes, blending with the rain into our skins.

Come on, my love, I thought. Let's go home.

We returned to the car as the rain began pouring fiercely down. We pulled away from the scene.

As I drove, the headlights like two ghosts rushing down the

tarmac, Putzi curled inside his blanket and silently kneaded the flesh of my stomach. I had visions of coming home at night to find him: cuddling in bed with him night after night, year after year, the two of us in our secret world. We could have our talks and no one would ever know what they were about. We would stay always in our balm of darkness, no one else knowing where we were or why. No one knowing of Putzi, my miracle child.

The rain sliced through the beams of the headlights like a cascade of splintering glass. The road became narrower, twisting tightly through the New England hills. I could see nothing beyond the immediate glow of the headlights; we might have been anywhere, at any time of history, in that darkness.

I looked down at my beloved Putzi again, kneading and pressing his soft lips to my stomach. He smiled. I ran my hand over his cool skin. I remembered, as in a faraway dream, the utter loneliness and desolation—unacknowledged, buried—I had felt in my other, daylight life: and the idea crossed my mind, riding on the waves of peace that lulled me, that perhaps it was possible—just perhaps—that a loneliness that was sufficiently deep, sufficiently all-encompassing and profound, might just, if one could imagine such a thing, reach out to another such loneliness, and the two together develop a transcendental power: if the lonelinesses were constant, never-ending, like an eternal lightless tunnel, could not the tunnels somehow meet, connect, grow beyond human limitation, until the melding had the capacity for almost anything—even this?

Was it not possible?

Then my thoughts broke off. I felt the tires skidding. I wrenched the wheel with the skid but the car soared out of control. There was an enormous scream of rubber on pavement, and other screams, all the screams in the world, and a sensation of impact as the car bounced from the road and Putzi's helpless flippers pushed desperately into me and a titanic monstrous tree rushed toward us. I heard glass shattering, shattering, shattering. Then I heard nothing at all.

4

I came to consciousness a day later in a New England hospital. I had felt as if I were struggling to free myself from some sticky gray soup; words would reach me occasionally, between long lapses of silent darkness; I could feel my body attempting to move; but it was not until later that my eyes opened and, through a haze of pain, I recognized the walls around me as those of a hospital room.

My midriff was wrapped in thick bandages and my left foot was in a cast. My hands were free; and I lifted them, the muscles complaining, toward my head. A bandage was wrapped around my temple as well. I tried to reconstruct what had brought me here; for a time I could remember nothing. Then, emerging as if from an oily pool, the image of Putzi materialized in my mind.

A deliriously happy nurse, a large woman with red hair, came to see me. I had had a severe concussion, she told me; I was now the proud owner of two broken ribs, a fractured ankle, and numerous abrasions on my head and legs. They had telephoned the university. Did I have any relatives who should be contacted?

I thought about it, then whispered: "No relatives." But I knew Anne and Ben would learn of my presence here somehow.

Sunlight streamed in through the hospital windows.

Later a highway patrolman entered the room, a skinny beanpole of a man. What could I recall about the accident? The amount of damage suggested I had been speeding; had I been drinking? You're lucky to be alive, ma'am.

"Yes, lucky," I whispered.

There was one peculiar detail which the patrolman felt he must clear up: at the accident scene that night, near the car, had been found the badly decomposed remains of a male infant. From the decayed condition of the body they estimated it had been dead for months, perhaps years. Did I have any knowledge of this?

I remained silent, staring blankly at the antiseptically white ceiling. Finally I offered a slight shake of the head.

"I thought not," the patrolman said, flipping his notebook closed and preparing to leave. "We figure it'd been dead out there a long time. Some mother abandoned it, maybe. We tried to get an ID, but nothing's come through. No missing infants anywhere in the area. Just a coincidence that your car ended up so close to it, I guess. Weird...Well." The patrolman thanked me for my time and left.

I stared unblinkingly at the ceiling, smooth as a pane of glass. Putzi, I thought: and the image of his frail body began to focus inside my mind. A vast hole seemed to open within me, widening with terrifying speed and engulfing all but my vision of the sunlit ceiling. The name ripped across my mind again and again. The room filled with angry morning daylight, glaring and mercilessly unforgiving. The name repeated, repeated; a voice I did not recognize whispered *Putzi, Putzi, Putzi.*

Although I still had some pain by January, I returned on schedule to my classes at the university. If my sister's husband ever noted the disappearance of an item from his trunk of school supplies, or if he ever connected it to reports of a long-dead infant found near the site of my accident, he never mentioned it to me. In any event, I have not seen either of them since my time in the hospital, and I rarely speak to them now. I find myself much too busy, what with two sections of Music History, two of Critical Theory, and numerous Master's and Ph.D. candidates under my supervision. Teaching takes up virtually all of my time; indeed, I've not returned to my monographs on unfinished music in months, and wonder now if I ever will.

Sometimes, on those rare occasions when I have a free moment, I might step into my bedroom when it is twilight outside and the room is suffused in a luminous peach glow. Occasionally I will sit at the side of the bed and run a dust cloth over the cello which sits perpetually, like a silent sentinel, beside it. Even more rarely I may take up my bow and stroke it a few times gently over the strings.

More often I will take a glass of wine, a single glass, and turn the stereo on to a low volume. I will sit absolutely motionless as through the speakers the chords and trills ring out clear and true: a Brahms cello sonata, say, or a Boccherini concerto.

Now and then I put on a recorded orchestration of Mahler's Tenth Symphony and listen with pleasure—at least until the opening of the final movement, when the funereal drumbeats are, as always, too loud and sharp. Gently, I want to tell them: gently: tap the drum so gently that the sound is little more, ultimately, than silence: and the two become, finally, all but indistinguishable. ◊

also from **Rock Village Publishing**
by **Edward Lodi**

Shapes That Haunt New England
(Ghost stories for the connoisseur)

Cranberry bogs...old stone walls...rural cemeteries...
an abandoned quarry...
the deserted dunes of Provincetown...
where the dead are not quite dead
ISBN 0-9674204-1-5   price $13.95

Haunters of the Dusk
(True New England Ghost Stories)

A ghost named Wendell... Blood-splattered walls...
The legend of Headless Alice... A relique from King Philip's War...
A tale of two graves... The house of the five suicides...
The old peculiar house... and other New England hauntings
ISBN 0-9674204-6-6   price $13.95

The Haunted Pram:
And Other True New England Ghost Stories

The restless spirit of a long-dead child...
a bible that flies through the air
(and the murderer who failed to heed its warning)...
a mysterious woman in a white dress... the ghost of a black dog...
pirates, their victims, and buried treasure...
a haunted quarry...
a mother's love that transcends death
ISBN 0-9721389-0-0   price $14.95

Murder on the Bogs:
And Other Tales of Mystery and Suspense

The quaint—and sometimes deadly—cobblestone streets
of New Bedford...
a lonely house near a cranberry bog...
a restaurant near an isolated dune on Cape Cod...
Boston's quiet (some might say, *too* quiet) Back Bay...
these, and other locales, for murder

ISBN 0-9674204-4-X   price $13.95

Cranberry Gothic:
Tales of Horror, Fantasy, and the Macabre

Familiar New England scenes—cranberry bogs, an old sea
captain's house, the Cape Cod Canal, and *your* backyard—
provide the settings for these stories of fantasy
and gut-wrenching horror

ISBN 0-9674204-9-0   price $14.95